F
AND

Anderson, Mary
  Who says nobody's perfect?   Delacorte
[c1987]
158p

Delighted when her "perfect" sister
Carolyn leaves for a year as an exchange student in Norway, Jenny is upset by the arrival of the beautiful,
brilliant, and popular Ingvild to take
Carolyn's place

  1 School stories   I T

ISBN 0-385-29582-0

Grades 10-12
87-5336
16749   12212   691468   © THE BAKER & TAYLOR CO.   0176

WHO SAYS NOBODY'S PERFECT?

Also by Mary Anderson

CATCH ME, I'M FALLING IN LOVE

DO YOU CALL THAT A DREAM DATE?

WHO SAYS NOBODY'S PERFECT?

MARY ANDERSON

DELACORTE PRESS/NEW YORK

Published by
Delacorte Press
1 Dag Hammarskjold Plaza
New York, New York 10017

Manufactured in the United States of America

First printing

Library of Congress Cataloging in Publication Data

Anderson, Mary [date of birth]
    Who says nobody's perfect.

    Summary: When Ingvild arrives in New York City from Norway as
an exchange student, she shares a room with fifteen-year-old Jennifer
who becomes jealous of Ingvild's beauty and popularity at school.
    [1. Jealousy—Fiction.   2. Self-acceptance—Fiction.
3. Students, Foreign—Fiction.   4. New York (N.Y.)—
Fiction]   I. Title.
PZ7.A5444Wh   1987   [Fic]   87-5336
ISBN 0-385-29582-0

To Ingvild and
Evy-Ann

WHO SAYS NOBODY'S PERFECT?

Chapter One

"My feet are *killing* me," groaned Liza as we met outside school. "I definitely can't go shopping with you, Jenny."

"You've got to," I insisted. "My sister's birthday is tomorrow and I still haven't gotten a present."

"So what? You can't stand her, anyway."

"I know that."

"Well, does becoming nineteen suddenly change a person or what?"

"Hardly. Carolyn will just be one year *meaner*, that's all."

I could tell Liza'd had a bad day, but I was still determined to talk her into going shopping. The thought of spending my hard-earned baby-sitting money on my sister was bad enough—I refused to do it alone. "I need to buy Carolyn something good, yet at the same time really rotten. You know?"

Liza pretended she wasn't listening. "Why'd we have to take gym again this year?" she grumbled. "Already I've got blisters all over my toes."

"That's because your sneakers are a size too small," I reminded her. "They always are."

"Naturally. Otherwise, my feet would look like surf-boards instead of skateboards."

Me and Liza had been friends for ten of our fifteen years, through ups and downs, highs and lows. In all that time I'd never noticed her feet were abnormal, yet she always insisted they were *huge*. Maybe it's some crazy fixation, like mine with Carolyn. Liza hates her feet and I hate my sister.

"I'm sweating, too," she complained, pulling her curly black hair into a ponytail. "I can't shop when I'm sweating, so count me out. Besides, what you just told me about that present makes no sense."

"It makes perfect sense if you let me explain. C'mon, let's get a soda."

I knew Liza real well. We'd argued so often, we could do it in our sleep. With a little more coaxing, I knew I'd talk her into going shopping. The only legitimate reason for refusing was a date, and I knew she wasn't seeing her boyfriend, Chuck, that day. He had a casting call for a toothpaste commercial. Chuck had gone up for a thousand commercials, but so far, he'd only gotten one walk-on. Still, Liza keeps hoping she'll be one of those Hollywood wives someday.

We pushed our way through the crowds gathered by the steps of Emerson High and finally got a whiff of fresh air. In September there's never any air in the classrooms. The board of education won't turn on the air-conditioning and the windows are permanently locked, so every year we suffocate until it gets cold again.

The street was really packed, as usual. That's because our school is near Broadway, just a few blocks from Lincoln Center, which is also near LaGuardia High School of

Music and the Arts, Professional Children's School (where Chuck goes), and Fordham University, plus two other public high schools. So around three o'clock every pizza parlor, hamburger place, and bagel store is overrun with starving teenagers. On nice days, kids hang out around the Lincoln Center fountain, eating ice cream and drinking sodas. Liza and I often stop there for a snack too. Of course, the primas only have yogurt and bottled juice—that's what the two of us call the ballet students who also hang out there, primas. All those girls are incredibly snooty and weigh under eighty pounds, half of which is hair.

Last year for a month, me and Liza pretended we were primas too—I mean, it seemed like a great way to meet guys—so we wore leg warmers and tights to school and dragged around big canvas bags filled with books and makeup and junk. We even glopped on tons of black eye shadow, which made us look like racoons. But it didn't work, we didn't meet anyone. I got a rash from the leg warmers and Liza got a backache from lugging that bag around. I still kid her about having one shoulder lower than the other.

As we walked up Sixty-third Street, I could see the fountain space filling up fast. "Indoors or out?" I asked. "We could go to Burger King or get sodas from the vendor."

"Outdoors, *please.* I *must* air my feet."

We bought two cokes from the sidewalk vendor, then found an empty spot on the big marble circle around Lincoln Center fountain. A million tourists are always crawling around there, spilling out of buses. Occasionally, you can see a Broadway star, a ballet dancer, or an opera singer too.

We dumped our books on the ground. Liza took off her sneakers, letting the fountain's spray cool her feet. "Explain yourself," she said, sipping her soda. "How can a present be both good and rotten?"

I knew she'd been listening. "It's part of my plan. This year I have to be more clever about Carolyn's present. Last year I bought her a tin of peanut brittle, which *she* knows *I* know she hates. Too transparent, see? Even Mom caught on. This year I have to be more subtle. It has to be a legitimate gift, but an insult too."

"Jen, if you'd put as much thought into schoolwork as you do into zapping Carolyn, you'd be brilliant."

"True. But who needs to be brilliant? Does my plan make sense?"

"Sure, I get it. I read something similar in a book recently. This guy breaks up with his girlfriend, and even though he now hates her, he buys her a present; something really tacky that he knows she'll think is gorgeous. He considers it poetic justice."

"That's it," I said. I really admire Liza's reading ability. She's always reading something, then relating it to everyday life. "Poetic justice, for another year of having to live with Carolyn."

"Well," she said thoughtfully, "maybe Albert could give you a poison beetle or something."

Liza loves making cracks about my boyfriend, Albert. He's heavily into ecology and animal rights, but he hasn't kept pet bugs in *years*.

"What's your mother getting her?" she asked.

"I don't know. It's some big secret. Mom never made such a fuss over *my* birthday."

Liza was about to take her socks off when she noticed

a security guard heading our way. Stuff like that isn't allowed around Lincoln Center. Guards on scooters ride around making sure no one is acting like a slob. Once I threw my leftover lunch into the azalea bushes, and a guard came over and chewed me out.

"Where were you planning on shopping?" she asked, quickly putting her sneakers back on.

"Macy's?"

"No way. These feet'll never make it to Macy's. Can't you find something lousy in this neighborhood? How much money have you got?"

"Ten dollars. That's a lot to throw down a rathole, I know, but it's the principle. I stayed up till midnight baby-sitting Eric Malone last night to earn the money."

"I won't sit for him anymore," said Liza. "That kid has insomnia. There's never any food in their fridge and their house is crawling with roaches."

"See how I've suffered? You've got to come along."

"Okay, we'll go to Macy's. But don't take forever. I've got tons of homework. Mr. Freeman expects us all to be Shakespeare scholars by next week."

The new school year was only a week old, much too early for me to be in the swing of things, and certainly too early for homework. I can't begin studying seriously until October. That's when I take out my calendar to mark off all the holidays. I like an airy school term, with lots of spaces between classes. Mom says I'll never get into a decent college with that attitude, but I tell her if that's the case I'll return to school when I'm forty, just like she did. Who needs brains, anyway? Carolyn has brains and she's still a dope.

"I don't like Mr. Freeman," I told Liza. "Teachers

who say 'we' make me barf. I came into class a little late this morning and he says, 'Do we have an excuse, Miss Beaumont, or do we think Shakespeare is unimportant?' Well of course he's unimportant—at least, he is at nine in the morning."

"He certainly can be a pain," Liza agreed. "Especially if he doesn't like you. Denise says he's a sadist who can smell fear. If he suspects you hate his class, he won't get off your back. Personally, I'm keeping a low profile until we've finished reading *Romeo and Juliet.*"

"It's too late for me; he has the scent."

Closing her eyes, Liza lifted her face toward the sun. "Jenny," she sighed, "don't you sometimes think life is incredibly repetitious?"

It's really eerie the way Liza can zero in on things. I mean, that was exactly the same thought I'd had all day. Here we were, living in the most exciting city in the world, so people say, during what are supposed to be our happiest years, so people tell us, and everything seemed so predictable and dull. There I was, planning how to one-up my sister for the millionth time, and there sat Liza with blisters, which she always gets because she always buys her sneakers too small. The vastly varied world around us hadn't affected our existence at all!

"Incredibly," I agreed. "I hoped becoming sophomores would change our lives, but we're exactly the same. I mean, we do and say the same dumb things."

Liza nodded. "I'm afraid we're just as immature as we were last year. Well, if we are, it's probably entirely our fault. We need to stretch ourselves, Jen, let new experiences enter our lives. For instance, know what my mom gave me for breakfast this morning? Cornflakes."

"You always have cornflakes."

"Exactly."

"We could try dying our hair again," I suggested. "I don't mean *green* or anything—I'm not ready for that. But maybe if we—"

"No, Jen, that's superficial, momentary. I'm talking about a real shake-up, you know? Like, what are you doing this Saturday? I'll bet you'll be with Albert, handing out animal rights leaflets outside Bloomingdale's, right?"

"I guess so."

"And I'll be with Chuck, listening to him tell me how he *almost* got a great part in a great show. Then on Sunday my folks will go to a concert, as usual, after which we'll have Chinese food for dinner, as always."

"And Mom will spend the weekend in the library, complaining that she'll never finish her thesis, just like she always does."

Liza sighed again. "It'll just be another year, Jen, same as the one before it. Like Shakespeare says, 'to the last syllable of recorded time.' "

"With you getting As and me getting Cs," I added. "Liza, you're making me feel *lousy.*"

"It's *life,* not me. Maybe if we were older, we could join the Peace Corps or something."

"No thanks. I don't want to spend my youth in some disease-ridden jungle, teaching people about toilets. Besides, you need skills for that, and I have none. Let's say we finish our sodas, then go to Macy's. While we're there, you could buy a pair of sneakers that actually fit—that'd be something different."

"Perhaps. Then maybe tomorrow, I'll have *toast* for breakfast."

Liza and I flashed our bus passes real fast, so the man in the token booth would think they were subway passes. Luckily, it worked. Getting on the bus would've taken forever and the subway only takes a few minutes.

As we pushed our way into the subway car, I kept thinking about what Liza had said. Was it possible to somehow change our dull, predictable lives? In the past few months we'd already changed our hair and makeup. Besides pretending we were primas, we'd also spent all of August exercising to Jane Fonda's video—until the arobics caused my downstairs neighbor's ceiling to fall in. But Liza was right: those were superficial things. We needed a *big* change. But where would it come from?

"Let's look for a sign," I suggested. "If something different happens within the next forty-eight hours, that'll mean this whole year will be different for us."

"You mean an *omen?*"

"I guess so. Does that sound nuts?"

"No. It'll open us to the possibility of change. Who knows? We might receive a sign."

There didn't seem to be any signs on the subway. It was noisy and smelly, same as always. Half the passengers looked as weary and the other half as mean and rotten as usual. And when we got to Macy's it was packed, as usual. First we checked out the food department downstairs. It's filled with the world's most luscious chocolates, all far too good for Carolyn. I considered buying her a mug with something nasty written on it, but nothing was nasty enough.

Upstairs, we checked through the silk scarves.

"Carolyn could wrap one around her neck and choke herself, just like Isadora Duncan," giggled Liza.

An accessory shop had interesting metal combs and manicure scissors. "Why not buy one of those," Liza suggested. "Carolyn might jab herself in a cuticle and bleed to death."

"No; death is too drastic. An insult is quite sufficient."

"How about toenail clippers? That's tacky."

A saleswoman passed the counter. "Can I help you?"

"Maybe," I said. "We were looking at those manicure scissors."

"*Nose* scissors," she corrected me. "They're only twelve dollars."

Liza and I stared at each other. *Nose scissors?* Then we burst out laughing. We were remembering the time I'd tweezed the hairs from Liza's nose because she said they were ugly. She nearly died from pain. Well, who knew there was such a thing as nose scissors, anyway?

Then the saleswoman showed us a hangnail nipper and an ingrown-toenail file. Eventually she realized we weren't interested and gave us a filthy look, like we were delinquents or something. She moved on to another, more "serious" customer.

"My feet can't hold out forever, Jen. Find something, fast."

We took the escalator upstairs to Books and Records. There were some dopey book titles Carolyn would've loved, but they were too expensive. (Since she's decided to become a psychiatrist, she reads the weirdest things.) Finally I found something: an English recording of *Romeo and Juliet.* It'd be the perfect present, because it was actually a gift for me. I could make a tape of it before giving it to Carolyn. That way, I wouldn't need to read the dumb play and I'd have a cultural gift, too, which only I would know was secondhand. Poetic justice, for sure.

"You've surpassed yourself," said Liza.

I was impressed too. "Now you can buy new sneakers," I suggested as I paid the cashier.

"No thanks. Acknowledging I have big feet is *not* the omen we're searching for. Let's just go home, okay?"

Chapter Two

That evening, the birthday mystery started mounting. Carolyn was hot to discover her present because not knowing was making her crazy. She can be real juvenile about things like that.

Every year Carolyn makes a list of things she wants, and Mom picks from it. Since our parents got divorced, Dad mails money, so that's no problem. But this year Mom insisted she had something special in mind, something not on the list.

"It's not like Mother to be so secretive," Carolyn complained as she paced through our bedroom. "She must've dropped some hint."

"Not to me," I assured her. "If she did, I was too busy to notice."

"Or too dense," she said. "Doing something unpredictable like this is out of character for Mother. I think studying for her M.S.W. has placed her under exaggerated stress. It's inhibited her normal reaction to things."

Trust Carolyn to make a big deal out of it. According to her, everything has a dark, hidden subconscious motive. If she doesn't become a psychiatrist, she can always get a job with the CIA.

"I have trouble relating to that theory," I teased, "because it's stupid."

"What would you know about theoretical analysis? Nothing! You've no conception of the pressures put upon premenapausal females forced back into the socioeconomic structure."

"Mom just wants to *surprise* you."

"I don't want a surprise, I want a word processor."

Carolyn had definitely become more obnoxious than ever. Her superflaky period began after she'd received an A + + on her last psychology paper. Getting As is nothing new for Carolyn, but after that she shifted her interest from infant psychiatry back to clinical psychiatry—which should make the babies of the world breathe easier.

Her term paper, "Depression in the Upper Latitudes," was about the high suicide rate in Scandinavian countries. Professor Maxwell called it "brilliant" and said she should study abroad. After that, she began to consider herself another Sigmund Freud. During the summer, she'd applied to universities in Sweden, Norway, and Denmark and been accepted as an exchange student. I thought it'd be great for Carolyn to study abroad—the farther away, the better. But with Mom back in school, too, that'd be too expensive.

"Girls, are you home?" I heard Mom calling from the living room. "Come help with packages."

I found her struggling with four grocery bags. "I stopped at Red Apple and got ingredients for lasagna," she said. "It's for tomorrow, but we'll have to make it tonight. Oh, and I ordered you a cake, too, Carolyn. French cream, your favorite."

"Don't make such a fuss, Mother. I thought we might go out and eat Chinese."

"On your birthday? Don't be silly. I always make dinner. Besides, we're having a special guest."

"What guest?" I asked. "We only have family on birthdays."

"Well, this year we're having a guest. But I can't tell you who, because it's part of my surprise."

Carolyn browned the ground beef and Mom began dicing onions. As I grated cheese, I heard Mom whistling. Mom *never* whistles. Could Carolyn be right? Mom *was* acting weird. (I hate it when my sister's sappy theories start making sense.)

Why all the secrecy? What could her special present be? And who was our special dinner guest?

Carolyn was in a state the next day when I came home from school.

"It's Professor Maxwell," she said, running around the kitchen like a nut. "I just got a call. At five thirty, I'm to put the lasagna in a three fifty oven. Isn't that odd?"

"It sure is. How'd your teacher know we're having lasagna?"

Carolyn put down the spatula she'd been holding for no apparent reason. "Jennifer, on this one day of the year, my birthday, I wish you'd cease your infantile behavior. You know very well I meant that *Mother* called. Professor Maxwell is my birthday dinner guest, but I can't imagine why. I don't think it's wise to socialize with an instructor. Transference is such an easy trap to fall into. I hope he doesn't feel obliged to bring a present."

What a lie! "When is he coming?" I asked.

"Six o'clock. I hope there's a decent wine to serve him. Why didn't Mother *tell* me? I've a million things to do."

"Like what? Dinner is already made."

"Like those slipcovers," she said, running toward the living room. "They're so depressingly dingy."

It was funny to see Carolyn so nervous. "Do you have a *thing* for this guy?"

She threw me an icy glance. "By 'thing,' I assume you mean an erotic interest. Hardly. Professor Maxwell and I are intellectually compatible. We have a mutual propensity for original theorizing."

That sounded like the old Mr. Spock mind meld. "The place looks fine."

She flashed me one of her superior looks, as if she were conversing with pond scuzz. "That's hardly an expert opinion, coming from someone who sleeps with cookie crumbs between the sheets. Let's at least fluff up these scatter pillows or something."

For the next hour, Carolyn raced around the house, making things look "decent." She even scrubbed the toilet bowl! Then she got out our best lace tablecloth and our best china and crystal, which hardly left enough time for her to slip into her best dress. When Mom came home, she was brushing her hair for the tenth time. "Why didn't you tell me earlier, Mother?" she asked breathlessly.

"That wouldn't have been a surprise. Relax, dear, Howard Maxwell *likes* lasagna."

"But why is he coming on my birthday?"

"You'll soon find out," said Mom, producing a bottle of champagne. "I think this will be festive enough."

"Hey, what's up?" I asked. "Are they announcing their engagement or something?"

"Mother, Jennifer's sophomoric comments are making me terribly uneasy."

"I *am* a sophomore," I said smugly.

I love needling my sister, but it usually has no effect. But this promised to be an unusual evening. I remembered my conversation with Liza. Might this be part of that omen we'd been waiting for? I couldn't figure what Carolyn's birthday had to do with our mutual rut, but I'd wait and see.

I was also curious to meet Professor Maxwell. When he arrived, I decided he was cute, in a dusty way. I mean, he was gray all over, gray suit and hair, as if he'd been buried under books too long. But he had a nice smile, so I decided not to hold the fact that he admired Carolyn against him.

"Come in, Howard," said Mom. Then she added, "The children don't suspect a thing."

A horrid thought hit me. Maybe *Mom* had a thing for this guy? After all, it'd been two years since her divorce, and she did date sometimes.

"I'm sorry your wife couldn't join us," she added.

"Yes, well September colds drag on forever."

That blew that theory. Carolyn's nerves were making me nutty, too—and awfully curious.

"This is Carolyn's sister, Jennifer," said Mom.

The professor extended a clammy hand.

Then Carolyn glided through the living room, acting ultracasual. "Professor, what a pleasure to see you. I hope you like Italian cuisine."

I hoped I wouldn't have to listen to her phony la-di-das all night.

But dinner went smoothly. Of course, Mom and Professor Maxwell spent the time remarking what an exceptional student Carolyn was. My sister pretended to be embarrassed, but she was actually lapping it up. I slumped into silence. That's what I always do when Carolyn becomes the hot topic of conversation. Sometimes, I get this eerie feeling in the pit of my stomach, like I'm shriveling up and shrinking away. I'm sure Mom doesn't deliberately try to make me feel inferior, but it's inevitable. There are so many good things to say about Carolyn and so few about me—academically speaking, especially. To others, Carolyn has always been like Mary Poppins, "practically perfect in every way," but it's loathsome living with a person like that.

Picking at my lasagna, I began thinking. Perhaps in some diabolical subconscious psychological way, Carolyn was the major reason for my present rut. After all, how could I be expected to grow, develop, and mature into an exciting, spontaneous, brilliant individual with Miss Perfection breathing down my neck?

By the time champagne and dessert was served, I'd managed to make myself quite gloomy.

Professor Maxwell noticed. "Jennifer, you've barely said a word."

"I'm the quiet type."

Carolyn laughed sarcastically. "Not when you're on the telephone with all your little teenage friends."

Who would've guessed she was still a teenager herself?

"We've prolonged the suspense long enough," said

Mom. "Let's take dessert into the living room, so Carolyn can open her presents."

I took my gift from the closet and placed it on the coffee table, while Mom and the professor kept grinning at each other. He took an envelope from his pocket and she put down a small, flat package, along with Dad's birthday card, which Carolyn opened first. It had cash inside, as usual. But there was also a message Carolyn read aloud: " 'I hope the exchange will be favorable.' I wonder what Dad means by that," she said.

So did I.

Mom grinned again. "Naturally, I told your father about my surprise."

"When is someone going to tell *me?*" Carolyn asked impatiently.

"Soon. First, open Jenny's present."

Carolyn was surprised by the record—I think she was expecting peanut brittle again. Luckily, she hadn't noticed I'd already slit open the cellophane wrapper. Anyway, it took her a minute to think of something nasty.

"Well . . . that's very nice, Jennifer. Of course, this isn't one of Shakespeare's greatest plays, is it, Professor? I haven't read it since I was a child in high school."

"You're welcome," I said.

"Now mine," said Mom excitedly.

Carolyn eagerly ripped the wrapping from the tiny package as we all held our breath.

Inside, there was an airline ticket—to Oslo, Norway.

Carolyn looked confused.

So did I.

"I don't understand," she said.

Neither did I, of course.

"My gift will help explain," said Professor Maxwell, handing her his envelope. "It's a letter of introduction to Professor Lars Martinssen at Oslo University. He's doing fascinating research on depression."

"Oh, I know. I applied there this summer."

He nodded. "And you were accepted, but couldn't go because of finances. Your mother explained all that. That's when we combined our talents in this scheme. You see, Lars Martinssen and I went to college together, and we've kept in touch. He'd told me he needs a secretarial assistant this term, preferably a student, for whom he and his wife will provide room and board. I wrote to say I had a talented premed student who'd already been accepted at the university but couldn't manage expenses, and he was interested."

Mom couldn't wait to tell the rest. "So you can go to Oslo after all. You'll be living with the Martinssens, which means you'll have no dorm expenses. You'll even get a little salary. You can study in Oslo, and it'll cost less than your tuition at Columbia."

Carolyn looked stunned. "I'm actually going to *Norway?*"

"Happy birthday, honey. I *knew* you'd be thrilled. It was really very simple, thanks to Howard. He pulled a few academic strings. After all, you'd already been accepted. The term just started, so you won't have much catching up. Howard assures me there won't be a language problem because most Norwegians speak English and . . ."

Mom kept talking, but I still couldn't believe what I was hearing. My sister was actually *leaving.* Pretty soon, there'd be an entire ocean between us. I'd have a room to myself and a life to myself at last. It may've been Carolyn's birthday, but *I'd* gotten the present.

"How long will she be gone?" I asked, trying not to sound too anxious.

"Until the end of the year at least."

Carolyn was overjoyed. "I can't thank you both enough. This is absolutely the best present I've ever had!"

"Wait," said Mom, "there's more to my surprise."

What more? I wondered.

"I hope Jennifer approves this part of our plan," said the professor. "Accepting Martinssen's terms made him view Carolyn much more favorably."

"Jennifer will love the idea," said Mom. "I'm in school all the time, so she'd be alone too much."

I'd lost the drift. "What plan?"

"Howard and I have arranged a mutual exchange. Professor Martinssen has a niece who lives in a small town outside Oslo. She applied for study abroad in the United States. So naturally, he thought if Carolyn stayed with him, then his niece could stay with us."

Offhand, that didn't sound so great. "You mean Carolyn can't go unless someone comes here? Who is this person?"

"That's the best part," said Mom. "It'll work out perfectly because she's a girl your own age."

My momentary vision of a room to myself went up in smoke. But Mom kept telling me what a wonderful cultural experience this would be, and how I could show this girl around the city—be a combination sister-guide-teacher, et cetera—and how I'd absolutely love it.

Carolyn looked nervous. "Of course she'll love it."

I quickly realized I held Carolyn's fate in my hands. If

I said no, her whole trip was off. I thought a minute. Should I bite off my own nose? No. I'd take Frankenstein in exchange for Carolyn.

Still, I didn't say anything right away. I let my sister's future dangle a while, savoring my sense of power. Actually, I never considered saying no. It *would* be fun to have a foreign exchange student live with us. I could show her the city, introduce her to American customs, all sorts of stuff.

Mom stared at me expectantly. "Well, do you approve the idea?"

"I guess it sounds okay."

She looked relieved. "I *knew* you'd think so. Everything has worked out wonderfully, almost as if fate had a hand in it. Right, Howard?"

"Yes, it's all mutually satisfactory, and Lars couldn't get a better assistant than Carolyn. In a few years, she'll probably be producing publishable material in the field herself."

Carolyn smiled demurely, sucking in another batch of compliments. I smiled, too, realizing that very shortly I wouldn't have to see her sappy face again until *next year.*

This absolutely positively had to be the omen I'd been looking for. I couldn't wait to call Liza and tell her the news.

Chapter Three

"What do you mean she'll be *living* with you?"

"Just what I said."

"Well, who is she? What's her name?"

"I didn't ask. Anyway, she's some professor's niece from someplace in Norway."

"When is she coming?"

"In a week or so, I guess."

Liza didn't sound thrilled. "What's wrong?" I asked. "I thought you'd be excited."

"Well, you said this was the answer to our rut. Frankly, I don't see how."

Liza was being dense. After all, she'd been the one to explain the ripple effect theory to me in the first place: when one drop of water falls into a pond, its ripples change everything.

I tried clarifying the situation. "Look, we're best friends, right?"

"Naturally."

"Then if my life changes, yours will, too. It's inevitable."

"It sounds like a pretty secondhand omen to me. Which reminds me, you'd better listen to that tape of *Ro-*

meo and Juliet you ripped off. Freeman is reviewing Act One in the morning."

"Who cares? Is that all you have to say about my stupendous news?"

"Look, whether it's an omen or not remains to be seen. At the moment, failing English is *not* the change I had in mind, so I'm boning up on Shakespeare. See you tomorrow, Jen."

Go figure Liza's attitude. Carolyn was *leaving.* Didn't she realize that changed the entire *world*?

I called Albert to tell him the news. "Guess what? My sister's going to Norway."

"What for?"

"To study Scandinavian depression."

"Oh. Are the Scandinavians depressed?"

"If they're not, they will be once Carolyn gets there."

Albert sounded equally uninterested. "That's nice. Listen, I ran off a new batch of flyers today, so we'll have lots to hand out this Saturday."

After months of standing outside Bloomingdale's each Saturday handing out animal rights petitions, I was bored. I longed for a *real* date for a change, but Albert was totally committed to the cause.

"Is that all you've got to say?" I asked.

"We'd better get there earlier this week. How about twelve?"

What was *wrong* with everyone? My world was changing and no one seemed to notice. Oh well, they soon would—once they saw what a dynamic personality I'd be, sans Carolyn. At last my life would soon start moving!

"I'll never be finished by Friday," Carolyn groaned. For a week, she'd been packing and making lists in her usual perfectionist manner: good winter woolens in one pile, casual, sporty things in another. It made me sick to see how organized she was.

"If only I could bring my skis," she sighed, "but my luggage is already overweight. I suppose I'll have to rent skis over there, but they won't be as nice, I'm sure. Swear you'll keep your hands off mine while I'm gone."

I swore. Carolyn and her boyfriend, John, both kept their cross-country skis stored in the basement. They were her prized possessions, which she waxed religiously between winter trips upstate. And they were the only thing I'd no desire to steal.

As I watched her pack, I kept hoping she'd leave behind a few choice items, like her cashmere sweater or linen skirt. Knowing what was on my mind, she left her closet clean as a bone. What she didn't pack she locked in the steamer trunk in the basement. When she'd finished, there wasn't a speck of lint left in her drawers. Mom thought it was considerate to leave so much space for the foreign exchange student. I thought it was rotten. She'd only done it so I couldn't borrow anything. Her side of the room looked more immaculate than ever, which meant my side looked even worse, if such a thing is possible.

"Jennifer, your untidiness is a fact of life, but I suggest you modify your behavior when your roommate arrives. I assume she's unaccustomed to living in a *hovel*. After all, you don't want her thinking of you as an Ugly American."

I started counting the days until her plane took off.

But there was still lots to do. Mom had to arrange for Carolyn's passport, which arrived just in time. Then Dad called from Seattle to say good-bye. And John came over for a farewell dinner. Carolyn's records and grades were transferred to Oslo University—Professor Maxwell took care of that. Mom checked the flight arrangements a dozen times, bought traveler's checks, et cetera.

And my foreign exchange student must've been doing the same thing on the other end. By now we'd received a letter telling us her name was Ingvild Larsen, from a small (unpronounceable) town, far outside Oslo.

"I looked the place up on the map," I told Liza, "but it isn't there. Anyway, I think it's someplace in the fjord country."

"This kid is starting to sound like Heidi."

"Well I hope she speaks English. What'll I do if I can't *talk* to her?"

"She must know some English or she wouldn't be coming, right? Besides, I think everyone in Norway speaks English. It's a second language or something."

"I hope so!"

To be on the safe side, I ransacked the house, looking for a pack of universal symbol cards that Carolyn had used for a psychology project.

"What do you need those for?" she asked.

"They're for Ingvild," I explained. "If we can't communicate, I'll use symbols."

"Don't be an imbecile," said Carolyn. "She's from Norway, not the *moon.*"

Mom smiled. "I'm sure Ingvild will speak English," she assured me.

Carolyn had a suggestion. "If you really want to communicate in a meaningful manner, acquaint yourself with

some of the Norwegian classics so you can have lively liter-
ary conversations. After all, this is a cultural exchange."

I now began counting the *hours* until her plane took
off.

Carolyn spent the entire day before she left on the
telephone, calling all her friends and classmates. It always
amazes me how many friends she has. Where'd she dig
them up?

"Professor Martinssen will be a marvelous mentor,"
she cooed into the receiver to I-don't-know-who. "I'm certain our collaboration will enhance our mutual awareness
on various psychiatric levels."

What garbage! She was going to type the guy's papers!

That day we'd received a telegram with the flight
number of Ingvild's plane, which arrived at Kennedy Airport on Sunday morning. I could hardly wait. Friday night,
Carolyn would fly out of my life, and on Sunday, Ingvild
would fly into it. Is that fate, or what?

Mom and John hired a limo to take Carolyn and her
luggage to the airport. They seemed surprised when I declined to go along. "I hate good-byes," I explained.

Mom didn't push the point. "We'll all be writing each
other constantly, I'm sure."

I tried looking slightly distressed so Mom wouldn't
think me weird. "Have a terrific time, Carolyn. Study,
study, study. Work, work, work."

"Oh, I intend to. I'll make everyone proud of me!"

When they'd gone, I walked through the apartment,
letting the reality of the situation sink in. For the next few

months, there'd be no heated dinner-table conversations revolving around sibling rivalry, schizophrenia, role reversals, overcompensation, and various other psychiatric mumbo-jumbo; no arguments about what I'd borrowed, what I'd ruined, what I should've done—and most especially, what was *wrong* with me.

At last I could stop competing with my sister and start becoming my own person!

Chapter Four

Liza kept arguing with me on the phone the next day. "Are you sure you want me to come along?"

"Naturally. We'll pick you up in the morning. We should meet Ingvild together. I know she's my omen because my life has already changed."

"How so?"

"This morning I cleaned my room."

"Impossible. I would've heard about it on the news."

"Know why I did it? Because Carolyn wasn't breathing down my neck, telling me I should. Remember that bracelet you lost last month? I found it under my bed."

"Terrific."

"Yeah, well I also found a sesame bagel, a half eaten brownie, and last week's math assignment. Do you think Mr. Bostwick would raise my grade if I handed it in late?"

"Too little, too late, Jen. Be thankful you didn't find maggots under there."

We arrived at Kennedy half an hour before landing time, just in case. Mom suggested I wear jeans, but I felt like dressing for the occasion, so I wore a red woolen skirt, which actually belonged to you-know-who. I found it in my closet when I'd cleaned. If only I'd stashed more stuff in there before Carolyn left, I'd have had my entire fall wardrobe.

"Let's get her gate number first," said Mom.

When we arrived at gate 17, Liza and I sat down to wait.

"We should've brought a sign with our names on it," I suggested.

"Calm down, Jen, we'll find her. Don't get so excited."

"Well, I *am* excited. In a few minutes, a *stranger* is coming to share my room."

"You've cleaned under the bed. Relax."

"But what if she's a weirdo, Liza?"

"You said *anything* is an improvement."

"Right. Well, what do you think she'll want to see first? It'll be my job to show her the city."

Mom could see I was nervous. "Take Liza's advice and relax. Ingvild will be here for months. The first thing we'll do is enroll her at Emerson tomorrow."

"Yeah, I suppose she'll have to go to school. How dreary." I checked my watch. "Shouldn't the plane have landed already? Maybe something's wrong. We should've brought those symbol cards, Mom, just in case. Or a sign, for goodness sake."

"Jennifer, why are you so nervous?"

I wasn't sure. I guess the whole thing had become a big prophetic deal to me. This seemed a chance to change my life around, and I was determined to like Ingvild, no matter what, even if she was mean, ugly, or stupid—though I hoped she wouldn't be too overly gross in any of those areas.

"She should've sent us a snapshot," I mumbled. "If there are lots of teenagers on the plane, we'll never find her."

At last, an announcement. SAS flight 210 had landed. As people began coming through the gate, I noticed lots of children, but no teenagers. Then Mom noticed a girl glancing around as if looking for someone.

"Could that be her?" she asked.

"Maybe," said Liza. "But she doesn't look at all like Heidi."

She certainly didn't. She was taller and much older-looking than I'd imagined—very pretty, with long straight blond hair. And very fashionable, too. She was wearing faded jeans, leather boots, and a terrific woolen sweater with reindeers: the picture of the healthy, outdoorsy type you see in travel ads for Scandinavia.

Mom went over to check and make sure. Ingvild smiled at us all, then we shook hands. "I'm happy to meet you, Mrs. Beaumont. And you, too, Jennifer."

Her English was great, and her accent made it sound even better. But she seemed so formal, it made me more nervous.

"Welcome to New York," I said. "This is my friend, Liza."

For a few minutes we stood around like saps, smiling and shaking hands. Finally Mom asked about her flight, which Ingvild said was fine. "I slept most of the way, so I will not have—uh . . ."

"Jet lag?"

"That's right."

We tracked down her luggage, then headed for customs. Ingvild didn't have much to declare, so it didn't take long. We left the airport and hailed a cab.

Ingvild glanced around expectantly. "So this is Manhattan?"

"Not quite," Mom explained. "We have to drive back into Manhattan. This is Queens, another borough."

"Queens?" she asked, making it sound real exotic. "I've never heard of this place."

"No one has," joked Liza.

Riding back into the city, I had a million questions to ask Ingvild, but I didn't say anything. Now that she'd actually arrived, I felt awkward. True, she didn't seem to be a beast or a weirdo, so that was in her favor, and true, Norway wasn't the moon. But it still seemed strangely foreign, and so did she. Liza and I stared at each other, we both stared at Ingvild, and I knew we *all* felt awkward.

Nearing Manhattan, Ingvild glanced out the window in amazement. "The buildings are so *tall.* There's nothing so big in Norway. In Oslo, we have a few office buildings, but nothing like this."

"Have you been to Oslo often?" asked Mom.

"Yes, but my home is far away from Oslo in the country."

At last there was something I could add to the conversation. "Hey, my sister's in Oslo now. At the university. She's staying with—oh, but you know all about that. Professor Martinssen is your uncle, right?"

"Yes. Oslo has a fine university."

"Will you be going there, too, someday?" asked Mom.

"Maybe. But maybe I'll go to college in America.

That's one of the reasons I am here: so I can plan my future."

Already thinking about college? She was definitely the serious type, which made me wonder if we'd get along. I mean, I could barely plan my *weekend.*

"You didn't bring much luggage," I commented. "I guess you'll want to do lots of shopping here, right?"

"No, I don't think so."

Uh-oh. If Ingvild didn't like *clothes,* we were in *big* trouble.

"But I did bring many musical tapes," she added.

Tapes? I hoped they weren't strange Norwegian composers I'd never heard of. "What kind of music do you like?" I asked.

"Many kinds. But I love Whitney Houston and Bruce Springsteen."

Liza perked up. "No kidding?"

"Don't you like them too?" she asked.

"Sure we do," I said, "but we didn't think you'd know about stuff like that in Norway."

"Oh, we *love* American music. And TV, too. Your show *Dynasty* is very popular. And we see all your movies."

I began to relax a little. Maybe Ingvild was a regular teenager after all, which meant I wouldn't be sharing my room with an alien.

"I was worried," I admitted. "I thought you wouldn't know anything about America. In fact, I wondered if you'd speak English."

"I wondered too," she confessed. "Oh, I knew you'd speak English, but . . ."

"I know what you mean." I laughed.

Mom smiled. "Well, maybe now we can all stop wondering and worrying and start getting to know one another."

Later that night, we had a real rap session. Ingvild hadn't heard the term, so Liza and I explained it. She quickly wrote it down in a little notebook, where she planned to keep a list of American expressions. She wanted to know everything and everything seemed to interest her.

First off when we'd arrived home, Ingvild noticed the closed-circuit TV in the lobby and asked Mom why it was there. Mom was a little evasive. I guess she didn't want to frighten Ingvild by explaining there are hundreds of bums, crooks, and junkies wandering around the city, just waiting to rip people off, so lots of buildings have sophisticated monitoring devices to keep them out. She merely said it was a "security convenience."

As the elevator took us to the sixteenth floor, Ingvild was amazed. "So many people in one building?"

"Sure," I said. "But you can live your whole life without meeting most of them."

When we entered our apartment, Ingvild noticed our view of the Hudson River and the New Jersey skyline from the window. "My little bedroom at home looks out over the lake. You can swim in this river?"

"Not unless you care to *die*," said Liza. "The Hudson is so polluted, it sometimes looks like a giant pudding!"

"Oh yes." She nodded. "Pollution."

Mom jumped into the conversation, eager to defend the Big Apple. "Isn't the view wonderful? The Circle Line tour boat passes by, and there's a boat basin for motorboats and yachts."

"Do you have a yacht, Mrs. Beaumont?"

Mom laughed. "We're not rich enough for that."

"On TV, everyone in New York seems very rich or very poor."

"At times I believe that's true, but actually most of us are somewhere in the middle."

"There are lots of poor people in the neighborhood," I added, "not to mention the Broadway crazies and the weirdos on the subway."

Ingvild looked nervous. "There is violence in this place called Central Park?"

"All foreigners think that," I told her, "but there's also rock concerts, tennis courts, lakes, and fireworks in the summer. Besides, I'll be taking you around, so you'll be fine."

She looked relieved. "I much appreciate that. I can see your room now?"

"Sure. C'mon."

Liza's mouth hung open as we walked in. "You really *did* clean up this place. I see you moved the dead elephant out of the corner."

Ingvild laughed.

"Maybe I'm messy sometimes, but I've decided to change my image. Ingvild, you can take the right-hand closet and this dresser. Oh, if you don't like my rock posters, you can take them down."

"No, I like rock music—but not heavy metal."

"Really? Me, too."

That's when the three of us began loosening up. First we compared notes about life in Norway versus life in New York. Lots of things were different. In school, they have *three* foreign languages; Ingvild took English, French, and German. And they also have a king, which is *very* different.

"Sometimes our mayor considers himself a king," said Liza, "but I guess that's not the same."

We talked about our families, too. Ingvild had three older brothers, which I said had to be better than having one cruddy sister. (I explained the word *cruddy,* which she quickly wrote in her notebook.) Naturally, it didn't take long to get on the subject of boys. She said most Norwegian boys were very athletic, skiing and skating in the winter, sailing in the summer.

"Boys don't do much of that here," said Liza. "Mainly, they hang out." Then she told Ingvild about her boyfriend, Chuck, who's going to Professional Children's School.

"Is it like on that TV show, *Fame?*" asked Ingvild.

"Sort of, but the kids don't dance around the streets like in the movie—they'd get hit by cars. Anyway, Chuck will definitely be famous, too, someday."

Naturally, I mentioned Albert and his passion for anything pertaining to nonhuman life.

"He sounds very interesting," said Ingvild.

"Do you have a boyfriend at home?" I asked.

"Many boys are nice, but . . . Well, I think maybe girls mature more quickly. Do you have mature boys at your school?"

Liza laughed. "At Emerson? Hardly. Oh, some seniors, maybe. But they never look at us."

"Why not? You're both so very pretty."

Me and Liza didn't argue. Instead, we talked about our friends. Ingvild wanted to know all their names and how often we saw one another.

34

"At home, it's different for me," she explained. "I only see friends in school or I must bike a long way to their houses. We live very far into the woods. My father is a carpenter. Sometimes he jokes and says that's why he needs to be near trees. To get to school takes me an hour by bus. Sometimes I must bring black bread and cheese because I get so hungry."

"You *are* like Heidi," Liza joked. "You know, Jenny spent days wondering what you'd be like."

"Well, I want to be just like American girls. So tell me more about your friends."

Liza mentioned Beryl Fleming, our most "celebrated" friend. Beryl had already been on the cover of a fashion magazine and done lots of other modeling.

"A model? Truly? Girls in New York lead wonderful lives. In a city like this, you must never be bored."

Naturally, I didn't mention we were usually bored to death. "Yeah, there's always something to do. And we'll do lots of it together."

We'd talked so long, we'd forgotten all about dinner. Liza had to leave for her weekly outing to the Chinese restaurant.

Before she left, Ingvild gave her a brief Norwegian lesson. *"Ha dat bra,"* she said. "That means, 'take care.'"

Mom and I decided to take Ingvild to the new Mexican restaurant which'd just opened. As we walked along Broadway, Ingvild was amazed to learn there were more than twenty restaurants to pick from in the neighborhood —Chinese, Mexican, Indian, Italian, and more. "In my whole town, there are only two restaurants. But I have eaten pizza and hot dogs, and I love them."

"Well, I bet you've never had a tortilla," I said.

We ordered some with chili. Ingvild pronounced it "very spicy, but good."

As we ate dinner I realized there were lots more subjects we hadn't yet covered—makeup, clothing, movies—it could take *months.*

That night as we got ready for bed, Ingvild combed her hair in the bathroom. She had gorgeous light blonde hair that went great with her pale blue eyes.

"Do you color it?" I asked.

"The sun does that. In summertime it gets almost white."

"No kidding. I thought color like that only came from bottles."

"Many Scandinavian girls have hair like mine. Do you color yours?"

"Yeah, I lighten it sometimes. Me and Liza like to experiment. Nothing too drastic, though. I mean, I wouldn't shave it off or anything. Oh, remind me to show you Gwen at school—she's half *bald.*"

"Such hairdos are popular in Norway, too. I think people change the outside when they can't change other things. Always my parents say I must try to improve the inside."

"Does it feel strange to be so far away from home?"

"Yes. But wonderful also," she said, beginning to wash her face.

"Don't you put anything on it?"

"My skin? No, nothing."

"Really? I never go to bed without slapping on tons of stuff—night cream, Noxzema, astringent, moisturizer. My skin's always too oily, too dry, or too something."

"Maybe I should try creams too. You think?"

"Why bother? You don't need them."

"Jennifer," she said, putting her things away in the bathroom cabinet, "I want us to be true friends—friends who share and tell each other things."

"Sure. So do I. We've already broken the ice—no, don't write that down, I'll explain it in the morning."

"I'm much worried about going to your school tomorrow."

"I'll show you the ropes—listen, I'll explain that in the morning too. I've got to perform my beauty treatments now, okay?"

As she left the bathroom, Ingvild kissed my cheek. "Thank you for my first day in New York. It has made me happy. And we will be true friends?"

"Naturally."

I glanced at myself in the mirror. I felt great. Sure, it'd be fun being the big sister for a change!

Chapter Five

Crummy Monday again—but this one wouldn't be as bad as usual. For once, there was a reason to go to school besides my rotten classes. Mom had given me the job of seeing Ingvild officially enrolled.

"Her school has already sent the necessary papers, so it shouldn't be a problem," she explained.

Even if it was, I didn't care. With any luck, we might sit in the office all morning—which meant missing English, math, and maybe even history.

We planned to catch an early bus. The night before Mom'd given me orders *not* to go on the subway. I guess she figured the sudden culture shock of loud noises, graffitti, and filth might be too much for Ingvild.

While we were dressing, Ingvild seemed awfully nervous. "Are you sure it's all right to wear trousers?"

"You mean jeans? Sure, kids at Emerson wear anything."

"Where will I put my costume I wear when I sleep?"

"Your pajamas?" Everything she said sounded so *cute*. "In that dresser. Usually I throw mine on the floor, but you're having a good influence on me."

"Yes? That's good. I hope the teachers at your school

will get satisfied with me. I make many wrong written words in English."

"So do I. Don't try to satisfy them, just try to survive —especially gym. That's the worst period of the day."

"Don't you like sports?"

"No way. Do you?"

"Yes, very much."

"No kidding. Well, never mind. At Emerson, you'll probably hate gym, anyway. I do. But maybe that's because gym teachers have to be subhuman to qualify for the job."

After we'd had breakfast, Mom said we should take a taxi to school instead of the bus—at least the first day. She'd decided Ingvild might freak out on *any* form of mass transit.

It certainly was a new experience, arriving at Emerson in a cab. I took Ingvild to the office and explained things. Mrs. Rosenfeld, the secretary, already had her transfer papers on file.

"Your grades are excellent," she said. "We've programmed you into all of Jennifer's classes."

I thought that was terrific because we could have lunch together. Things had gone so smoothly, we'd only missed twenty minutes of English—unfortunately. I introduced Ingvild to Mr. Freeman, who assigned her a seat near mine. Naturally, I hadn't done my homework, but at least I had a decent excuse for once: "Yesterday, we had to go to Kennedy and then customs and then we—"

"*All right,* Jennifer. Please open your book to Act Two, Scene One. Ingvild, are you familiar with this play?"

"*Romeo and Juliet?* Oh, yes."

"Fine. I'm sure all my students join me in welcoming

you to our country and our class. If you have any trouble understanding the play's language, see me after school; I'll be happy to clarify things for you."

There was nothing worse than having Freeman "clarify" Shakespeare. He had the uncanny ability of making everything—including teenage lovers, poisonings, and death—dull. I spent most of the period ignoring him, as I made up an itinerary for Ingvild. Where would we go first? What should I show her? I hardly knew where to start.

During study period I chaperoned Ingvild around school and introduced her to the kids and teachers. Everyone said welcome and lots of people stopped us in the hall. Clifford Fudjinski didn't lose any time coming on to her. Cliff considers himself a heartthrob, though mine has never skipped a beat for him. That's because he's dead from the neck up.

"What country you from again?" he asked.

"Norway."

"Terrific." He shifted his weight from side to side, trying to look intelligent, a totally useless effort.

Ingvild was very polite. "Your name is hard for me. I can't speak it. In Norway, most everyone has a Norwegian name."

"Oh yeah? Here, most everyone doesn't."

"Sorry to interrupt this scintillating conversation, but I have to get Ingvild to French before the bell."

"Where'd you say you got her from?" he asked.

"She's a foreign exchange student, Cliff. I traded her for my sister Carolyn."

"No kidding. I've got a brother I'd like to trade. Can

I get a girl in exchange too? Hey, I'll settle for anything—a *dog* or something."

"Nice talking to you, Cliff," I said, guiding Ingvild down the hall. "Definitely not the mature type, right?"

"Right," she agreed.

Mrs. Hirsch, the French teacher, was thrilled to get a foreign exchange student in her class. She spent ten minutes telling us how she'd been an exchange student herself and had spent a year in Paris as a teenager. Ingvild seemed interested, but the rest of us had heard that a million times already.

When it was time to read aloud I tried melting under the desk, as usual. My French is on a par with Miss Piggy's and my accent is worse. Luckily, she called on Ingvild instead. She read a whole paragraph and pronounced everything perfectly.

"Excellent," said Mrs. Hirsch, "you'll be a great addition to our class."

"Where'd you learn to speak like that?" I asked enviously.

"I have a good ear, I think."

"I have *no* ear."

"Maybe we two will do language together? I will teach better French and you will teach better English."

"Throw in better homework and it's a deal."

Next was lunch period. I couldn't wait to get to the cafeteria and show Ingvild off to everyone. "Don't worry about the creeps and ditzoids. I'll steer you clear of them," I assured her.

Ingvild stopped, anxious to write *ditzoid* in her notebook. "Sometimes I hear these words in American cinema, but no one explains them."

"Ditzoids are worse than creeps," I explained, "and we have our share of both at Emerson. But there are great kids too. This year we have a super lunch table. Last year I worried lots about stuff like that. In fact, last year I felt practically invisible around here. Except once, when I made a fool of myself—then *everyone* noticed. But lunch tables are awfully important, don't you think?"

"Yes. To be with friends is important."

The cafeteria was filling up fast as we took places on line at the food counter. I looked around for Liza and Albert but couldn't find them. I noticed Lara, Donna, and Kim seated at a nearby table. "Speaking of ditzies," I whispered to Ingvild, "the Terrible Three over there are a perfect example."

"The Terrible Three?"

"Yeah, those girls over there. That's what me and Liza call them. They must think they're triplets because they're always together. The cheese has definitely slipped off all their crackers."

Ingvild began writing again. "They are—ditzoids?"

"The worst. Kim's father is a rich lawyer, but she'll only wear rags. See? Everything she wears is ripped in ten places. Not trendy Fiorucci rags either—*real* rags. Donna is even nuttier. She says she's the reincarnation of a horse in a painting at the Metropolitan Museum. And Lara is altogether spacey. Maybe she's popped too many pills or pierced her ears too often. Anyway, I'd steer clear of them."

"At my school, we also have a girl who is strange. She always wears black leather. She says her father is a famous Norwegian film star. It's very sad. Some things aren't so different in Norway."

By now, we'd reached the front of the lunch line, and I was trying to see what looked vaguely edible.

"Jennifer, I have only some kroner and traveler's checks. I haven't been to the bank."

"Don't worry, Mom gave me lots of money. It should be a crime to charge for this garbage anyway. They never have anything decent, but I'm too lazy to bring lunch from home."

"Then maybe I will make us lunch tomorrow."

"Sounds great. Mom's always too busy. This year she has a part-time job in a real estate office, plus going to school."

"Then I will help in your house. I don't mind cooking."

"I *hate* it. I can't handle a recipe with more than five ingredients."

Liza was already seated at our table when we got there.

"I cheated," she explained. "I sent Larry on line for my lunch. I couldn't stand for another *second*. I hope by next week these sneakers will be broken in."

"You have sore feet?" asked Ingvild.

"No, by now they're *numb*. How'd you like your first morning in our booby hatch?" Naturally, Ingvild wrote that down, along with the explanation.

"Very good," she said. "Your school is much bigger than mine. At home we have only three hundred pupils. Jennifer has already helped me meet many people."

"And I've told her who to keep away from, too," I added, gesturing toward the Terrible Three.

"Yes," agreed Ingvild, "you're a very good sister."

It was great getting a compliment like that. My real-life sister would die before she said a thing like that. "I've made a list of things to see. After school, we might visit South Street Seaport, or go shopping on Fifth Avenue."

"Yes, I want to see many things. My parents say I must learn everything. But I must also study. Today, I wish to see Mr. Freeman to talk about the play. There are many English words I don't understand."

"*No one* understands that stuff," I said. "English like that hasn't been spoken for centuries—'leige,' 'knave,' 'forsooth,' and all that junk are *ancient.* Ditch your work and let's go sightseeing."

Liza agreed. "One talk with Freeman and you'll be *totally* mixed up."

By the time Vivian and Albert arrived at the table, lunch period was half over.

"Something exploded in biology," Albert explained. "Mr. Finch made us mop it up."

I could see Albert was in a rotten mood, not only because of the explosion but because I hadn't called him on Saturday to cancel out. I'd been too busy planning for Ingvild's arrival. I tried apologizing, but he wasn't in the mood.

"I had *five hundred* flyers, Jen. I could've signed up tons of people if I'd only had help. Every day, seals are being bopped over the head. Don't you care?"

Albert and I often had blowups about that subject, and I sensed a beaut coming on. I'd tried getting involved in his animal rights causes. Really. Only sometimes on a Saturday, I felt like going *inside* Bloomie's, instead of always standing outside, slaving to get signatures.

"If only some other kids would help," I complained. "Maybe then it wouldn't be so bad."

"Saving animals sounds important," said Ingvild. "Maybe someday you will take me to stand outside this store?"

"Are you *volunteering?*" asked Albert in amazement. He'd already cornered everyone in school, but it was always no go.

"Careful, Ingvild," I cautioned. "Signing up with Albert is slave labor: nothing an hour, time and a half for overtime."

"Don't mind Jenny," he said. "You must be the foreign exchange student from Norway, right? Do you realize your country is responsible for a major part of the seal slaughter?"

Ingvild blushed. "No. I'm sorry."

Larry and Vivian arrived with lunch trays and sat down.

"*Can* it, Albert," said Liza. "The girl has only been in our country a few hours. Don't dump a guilt trip on her."

"We're *all* guilty if we don't *do* something about it," he argued.

I jabbed him in the ribs. "Be *nice* to Ingvild," I muttered. "That's an order."

Honestly, Albert could be heavy going at times. If he weren't so cute, dedicated, and intelligent, I might not like him at *all.*

Luckily, Beryl breezed by to lighten up the conversation.

"I can't stop for long, gang. I'm off to the principal's office for an early dismissal pass. I've got a job from two to five at Bloomingdale's. I'm their Lovey Face girl today. Isn't that *marvelous?*"

"I guess so," said Vivian. "What's it mean?"

"Lovey Face is a new line of teenage cosmetics. It comes in dreamy frosted pink bottles. I think I'm supposed to spritz and spray people with it as they walk by."

"Spray is right," said Larry. "My sister bought some of that stuff, and it should be used on bugs."

Beryl failed to see the humor. "Lovey Face is a class product, only sold in the finest stores." She finally noticed Ingvild. "Who's the new addition to our table?"

I made the introduction. "This is Ingvild Larsen. She's an exchange student from Norway."

"Oh sure, you told me all about her. I guess I've been so busy, I forgot. Hi, Ingvild. Your name sounds so—well, *Norwegian*. So Jen, what've you done with Ingvild so far? I've only got a sec, but tell me all about it."

"She just got here yesterday," I explained.

"But I've been to a Mexican restaurant and I've met many American pupils and teachers," said Ingvild.

Beryl checked her makeup and combed her hair. "Jennifer, you simply must liven up this girl's schedule. A trip to the new boutiques is essential. Oh, and I have the perfect thing for you to do this afternoon: come to Bloomie's and watch me in action. There's also a big fashion show. Enrico is a marvelous new designer who's introducing his winter line. You'll love it."

By now, Ingvild must've thought Bloomingdale's was definitely where all the action is. "Many things happen at this store?"

"It's the city's heart," said Beryl dramatically.

"Well, I *wanted* to take Ingvild shopping today," I said.

"But Ingvild wants to study Shakespeare," said Liza.

Beryl couldn't believe that. "You're not serious? You

can study anytime; what's the rush? After all, Shakespeare's been dead for years. You didn't cross the Pacific Ocean just to read a book!''

"The Atlantic," Albert corrected. "Don't make any plans for Ingvild on Saturday. She's already offered to help us with our petitions, hasn't she, Jenny?"

"That's taking advantage of a foreigner," said Vivian. "She should go to the Norwegian Consulate and complain. You'd rather see a Giants game or go to Chinatown this weekend, wouldn't you, Ingvild?"

"Oh, I want to do *everything*. Maybe Shakespeare can wait. Let's go to Bloomingdale's."

"Fantastic," I said. "It's been ages since I've been *inside*," I added in a cool, sarcastic tone, looking directly at Albert.

Beryl patted lip gloss on her mouth. "A wise decision. Incidentally, Ingvild, I *love* your sweater. Calvin Klein is charging a fortune for those this year. But I guess hand-knit woolens are much cheaper in Norway, right?"

"This was very cheap. I made it myself."

"You *made* that?" I asked. "How long did it take?"

"Not long. I can teach you. Knitting isn't hard. My grandmother taught me."

Beryl was impressed. "I hate to tell you what I paid for a sweater just like that last week: an entire day of modeling, that's what. Listen, maybe we can all get together someday so Ingvild can give us all a knitting lesson. Or we could have a knitting party."

Liza nearly choked. "A *knitting* party? Are we in a *time warp*?"

"It was only a thought," said Beryl lightly. "Don't girls in Norway do things like that?"

"No," I said, winking at Ingvild. "Most of them listen to Bruce Springsteen. Norway isn't on the *moon,* you know."

"Oh. Then let's forget it. I've got to dash. See you later, guys."

"I like your friend," said Ingvild. "She's very . . . *colorful.*"

Then came dreaded *gym*. I'm thankful it's my last period of the day, so I can cut it whenever possible. But I couldn't be a bad example for Ingvild, so I gritted my teeth and pushed open the gymnasium door. As usual, all the atheletic types were already in there, throwing the old volleyball around, while the few girls who loathe contact sports hung in corners staring at the ceiling.

You should hear the excuses we come up with, *not* to get in to a game. I was hoping my allergy excuse would last me through the year, if I could keep sneezing and itching until June.

Gym is one part of the day Emerson boys aren't interested in Emerson girls. They consider it a punishment to share the gym with lowly females who they assume can't kick or throw and just take up space. Most guys are busy being macho hoping to make girls feel stupid.

The girls have a volleyball team and the guys mostly play basketball. Actually, very little playing ever gets done during gym. By the time the teacher calls the role, the period is half over. What a total waste of time. I mean, I wouldn't mind if we'd exercise, or something *useful*. Sitting on the sidelines hardly helps tighten up my thighs!

But Ingvild was anxious to get into a game. "I love sports, Jennifer."

"Okay, I'll talk to Ernestine; she'll probably get you in."

Ernestine Matthews was nearly six feet tall and the best player at Emerson. She'd already helped the school win lots of games and was always looking for "new blood," so she let Ingvild try out.

While they pounded the ball back and forth, I put on my usual long face (signifying pain) and approached Mr. Farley, our gym teacher.

"I think I pulled a muscle."

Farley hardly bothers listening to my sappy excuses. Some girls pretend they have cramps, backaches, head-aches, and hangnails the entire *year.* "Okay, Beaumont, sit this one out."

I found a seat by the wall where the other "chronics" were hiding. Liza was one of them.

"Why'd you come so late?" she asked.

"I couldn't face it. It's been a decent day so far and I hated to ruin it."

She massaged her leg. "I actually tried getting a bas-ket. I'll never do *that* again. Hey, look at Ingvild. She's actually *playing.*"

"Yeah, she says she loves sports."

"Well, don't hold it against her. Nobody's perfect."

We watched Ingvild jumping around, wacking that volleyball back and forth.

"Come play, too," she shouted over at us.

I mouthed the words *I'd rather die* at her. I think she got the message.

After a while, Ingvild came running over. "I'm being put on the team. Ernestine said I might play in a game soon. Isn't that good?"

Personally, playing ball against another high school while everyone watches and shouts "Hit it, lead-legs!" wasn't my idea of fun. No matter how skinny girls are, their rear ends always seem to wobble. All thing's considered, I'd much rather stick my head in an oven.

"Sure, Ingvild," I said, smiling. "That's terrific."

Chapter Six

We took the subway to Bloomie's. After all, Ingvild would have to do it sooner or later, right? Actually, it didn't turn out to be that bad. I prepared her for the dubious experience.

"New York City subways are incredibly noisy and disgustingly dirty," I explained, "but if they don't break down, they're also awfully fast."

During the ride, she wondered about one thing. Since most of the windows were sprayed with graffiti, how would we know when to get off?

"Relax," I assured her, "I know this route by heart."

What a pleasure to arrive at Bloomingdale's without a stack of petitions for a change! Getting to see things through Ingvild's eyes was fun too. She stared at the lights, black marble, mirrors, brass, and gold as if I'd brought her to a palace.

"We have no stores like this at home," she sighed.

"When I die, I think I'll be buried in here, somewhere near the overpriced denim jackets or designer jeans. Anywhere between Calvin Klein and Ralph Lauren's stuff would be fine. Or maybe by the makeup counters," I added.

On our way to the third floor, we both drooled at everything. "Don't bump into any mirrored walls," I cautioned. "They can be killers."

We found Beryl inside one of the boutiques, spraying Lovey Face on shoppers' wrists. She was wearing an oversize baby pink sweatshirt, pink cotton sweatpants, and tons of trendy pink wooden bracelets. She kept parading up and down the aisles, carrying a large sample bottle of perfume.

"What a nice way to meet people," Ingvild observed.

"And get rich, too. Beryl makes a *fortune* modeling."

"She'll be able to go to a very fine college."

That was a laugh! "I don't think that's part of her plan. When Beryl is eighteen, she'll probably be on the cover of *everything*."

"She'll still need a good education, no matter what she does. My parents always tell me that."

I didn't argue that point because I was more interested in getting a whiff of the perfume Beryl was peddling.

"Hi, guys," she said brightly, then sprayed some mist in our direction.

"Interesting," I said. "How much?"

"Only twenty dollars, at the Lovey Face counter downstairs."

"Too much, though it might clear up my sinuses."

"Too strong?" asked Beryl. "Their ad says it's a combination of a spring shower and summer rain."

"Maybe a dog got caught in that shower."

Beryl spritzed some on Ingvild. "What do you think?"

"It's very sweet," she said politely.

Beryl nodded. "Frankly, I don't like it either, but the bottle is *adorable.* I love the little angel on top."

"They should've spent less on the outside and more on the inside," I suggested.

"True, but some customers really go for it. I guess you can sell anything if it has the right image. And speaking of that, Jenny, I just found out a fascinating fact. Lovey Face plans to spend a small fortune promoting this stuff. They want to create a Lovey Face girl, for their magazine campaign."

"And you're going to be it, right?"

"Don't I wish! Unfortunately, they're looking for a *new* face, which means a nonprofessional."

"Isn't *your* face new enough?" asked Ingvild innocently.

"No," she sighed, "I'm already considered overexposed. Anyone already signed with a modeling agency is *out*.

"Oh, that's too bad," I said.

"But my bad luck might be your good fortune, Jenny. I think *you* should try out for it."

I won't pretend I'd never thought of modeling, because I had—lots of times. In fact, Beryl had offered to take me down to her agency for an interview, but I'd always chickened out. At the last minute, I'd get a pimple or break out in hives or something equally disgusting. But since Carolyn had left—which meant there was no one to tell me what an incompetent slob I was—my attitude had suddenly improved. "Do you really think I should?"

"Sure. Naturally, Lovey Face will be interviewing lots of high school girls, but I think you stand a good chance."

Ingvild agreed. "You're so very pretty, Jennifer. Yes, you *should* try."

Beryl interrupted the conversation to spray a few customers passing by. "Look, I don't know all the details yet, but the company starts interviewing girls in about a month."

"What would I have to do?"

"Well, there's usually a photography session, with tons of pictures. Mainly, you'll have to show confidence. Being self-assured is a model's most important asset—even more important than good looks. Sometimes, *thinking* you're beautiful is actually better than *being* beautiful."

I tried treating the whole deal casually, but I must admit I had a fleeting image of my face slapped on a million magazine covers. "Okay, maybe I *will* try."

"Terrific. I've got to go now, guys. Work, work, work. I must keep spraying until five o'clock. They don't pay me for just being charming, you know. Before you go, check out that fashion show I mentioned. I heard it's marvelous." Beryl breezed down the aisle, spraying everyone in her path.

Ingvild and I went to the fourth floor to catch the premiere of the winter line by Enrico, the hot new designer. Toothpick-thin models paraded around in stuff which looked like it'd been made from old horse blankets, complete with hats that looked like feed buckets.

Ingvild's mouth fell open. "Do people in New York wear such things? Would *you* wear them, Jennifer?"

"Not in this lifetime. I think Enrico must have a few loose screws."

"Only nineteen hundred dollars," said the fashion announcer, "complete with saddle pouch shoulder bag."

We burst out laughing. "C'mon," I said, "let's check out the freebies downstairs."

On the first floor we passed the makeup counters,

helping ourselves to the free tester samples. I tried Revlon eye-shadow, a pink Halston lipstick, Ralph Lauren cologne, and a mess of other stuff, until my face weighed ten pounds.

Ingvild tried experimenting, too, but didn't like the results. "I think it makes me look like a clown. When I put on mascara, my eyes stick shut."

"You don't apply it properly," I told her, "but I'll teach you."

She tried a peach lipstick called Summer Evening. She pressed her lips together then stared in the mirror. "I think Bloomie's is wonderful. When I die, *I'll* come here, too."

Next, we went back upstairs to try on boots and shoes. I found a great pair of beige heels in soft, buttery suede that cost a hundred dollars; but it didn't cost anything to try them on. Then we checked out Norma Kamali's padded dresses, in which I looked like a linebacker.

Finally, a saleswoman inquired if we needed help.

"No, thanks," I said. "I'm afraid all your merchandise is dreadfully tacky." Then I motioned Ingvild toward the escalator.

"Weren't you rude, Jennifer?"

"Oh, Liza and I do that all the time. You've got to act snooty to the sales help or else they treat you like dirt. Take my advice and always be a little rude in New York. Otherwise, people take advantage of you."

"Really?" she asked, staring at me with admiration.

"Sure. Stick with me and you'll be a true New Yorker in no time." I really did feel like a big-sister-tour-guide— not a bad combination. But it was time to leave. "Mom'll be home at seven thirty and there's no food in the house. When Carolyn was here, the three of us took turns making dinner, so now I'm doing double duty, and I'm a *rotten* cook."

"Shall I make dinner tonight?"

That sounded great. Tuna casserole and omelets, which even *I* don't like, are my only recipes.

When we got off the subway, I took Ingvild to the Food Emporium on Broadway. She was just as impressed with it as she had been with Bloomingdale's. The Emporium is a neighborhood supermarket where you can buy anything from fresh flowers to live lobsters, and everything in between.

"Buy anything you like," I said, "the only thing I truly hate is beans."

"Me, too. Isn't that interesting?"

Come to think of it, who likes beans?

When Mom arrived home, dinner was already on the table. Ingvild had made pork chops with lemon sauce, salad with fresh dressing, and potatoes au gratin.

Mom was delighted. "Ingvild, you did all this yourself?"

"Oh yes. It's a simple meal, but I didn't have much time. Jenny took me to Bloomie's."

As we ate, Ingvild told Mom all about her day. She'd liked school and all my friends, she'd loved gymn, and she'd found the subway "very interesting."

"Jennifer, you've taken Ingvild on the subway *already?*"

"Relax, Mom. Ingvild's a real New Yorker now. She's seen Bloomie's and the subway: the best and the worst of things."

"Tell your mother about Lovey Face," said Ingvild.

"Who's that?"

"Oh, it's a new product Beryl is pushing."

"Yes," said Ingvild excitedly, "and maybe Jenny will —'push' it, too."

I tried not to get too carried away as I explained the whole deal to Mom. "I suppose it's a chance in a million, but maybe I'll take it."

"If Beryl thinks you have a chance, you probably do, dear."

"I think she has a wonderful chance," said Ingvild. *"Anything* can happen in New York!"

As we finished eating, I suddenly realized a tremendous change had taken place: the voice of doom had left our dinner table. If Carolyn had heard my news, she would've smashed it with a sledgehammer. She would've given me the whole psychological number: don't raise your hopes, exceed your capabilities, overreach your physical capacities, et cetera, et cetera. For the first time in my life, there was *no one to put me down*. What a great feeling.

Ingvild served fresh fruit salad for dessert. I offered to do the dishes.

"Aren't you going to wait for me to *force* you?" asked Mom.

"Not tonight. I'm a new person, Mom. Haven't you noticed?"

"Does that include doing homework?"

"No, I wouldn't go that far."

"I could help you with French," offered Ingvild. "And you can help me with the words in the play."

"Okay," I agreed, "but you're getting the worst of the deal."

"And when we finish, I will write my parents. I will tell them all about my first two days in New York.

"Don't mention our subways just yet," said Mom. "Okay?"

Later that night, Liza called. "How was Bloomie's?"

"Terrific. Ingvild loved it. She loves everything about New York. I always told you it was a great place, Liza. How could you think it was *dull*?"

As the week continued, Ingvild settled into the routines at Emerson. Every day she met more students, and everyone liked her. Chaperoning her around school made my classes seem less deadly. It was fun showing her off to friends and introducing her to teachers: it made me feel responsible, and I liked that. Also, the fact that she was a good student rubbed off on me. The teachers, even the ones who despised me, saw me in a new light. I wasn't just that-dumbo-in-the-first-row, I was now the girl who'd brought an exchange student into school—and *any* change in a teacher's attitude would've been an improvement for me.

But my chaperoning job didn't last long. Ingvild soon made friends on her own. She talked to everyone and *anyone*. She met the nerds, the jocks, the brains—even the Terrible Three. Ingvild had met more people in one week than I had my first *year*.

"How'd she get so popular so fast?" asked Liza. "You suppose it's her accent?"

"Maybe. Whatever the reason, I'm glad. I wouldn't want to be blamed for introducing a dud into the group."

But no one complained. In fact, some brainy sopho-mores had formed a study group which met at a branch library after school. They asked Ingvild to join. She asked me to come along, too, but I declined. "No thanks, Ingvild, I don't fit in with brainy types. I think I'm allergic to them."

By Thursday, we'd finished *Romeo and Juliet,* and Mr. Freeman gave a written test, on which I got my usual C. Ingvild got B minus, which meant she'd done lots more studying than *I* had.

In honor of Ingvild joining the class, Mr. Freeman then assigned us Henrik Ibsen's play, *A Doll's House,* because "I think we should explore some of the great literature of Norway, now that we have a student with that cultural background."

Mom was interested in culture too. She bought us tickets to the Metropolitan Opera's production of *Aida.* The sets and costumes were great, but all those people carrying swords and singing while dying didn't make much sense. I'm sure the ancient Egyptians never did that stuff! Ingvild said she loved it, but I bet she would've preferred a rock concert, same as me.

That Friday in biology, Mrs. Lambert screened a movie about chicken embryos. I sat in the back, tuned out, as usual. I was taking notes—not about biology, but about my improved condition. Since Carolyn had departed, there'd been lots of changes, so I made a list:

1. Ingvild had brought very few clothes, which meant more closet space for me.

2. Ingvild was a naturally neat person, so she loved cleaning our room.

3. Ingvild was a good cook, which meant tuna casserole less often.

4. Talking to Ingvild before going to sleep was better than constantly fighting with Carolyn.

No doubt about it: my life had definitely improved.

That night, Albert called to remind me of our weekly "date."

"We'll meet at twelve o'clock, sharp. And don't forget to bring Ingvild."

"Only if you promise not to *bully* her, okay?"

I told Ingvild she didn't need to come along. "Sometimes petitioning can be a real pain."

"I'd like to help the animals, Jennifer. At home we have many pets. Some live in the house and many live in the woods. In the woods, we have many rare types of birds."

"Really? Well, tomorrow outside Bloomie's, I bet you'll meet some rare types of New Yorkers."

Chapter Seven

"Save the seals. Sign our petition to save the seals."

It was only one o'clock and I was already hoarse. On a typical Saturday, I usually don't lose my voice until three o'clock. But Fifty-ninth Street was more crowded than usual, so I had to shout even louder.

Albert was in fine crusader form. As the wind blew through his curly brown hair and the sun hit his aviator glasses, he shouted, "Don't shop until you stop," corralling people toward us. As always, we'd brought along a card table, where we'd set up our petitions, a large cookie jar for donations—to be taken to the Humane Society—and lots of animals rights buttons, which we sold for a quarter each.

At first, Ingvild was too busy trying not to get trampled to be of much help.

"We shouldn't have brought her," I said with concern. "These crazy crowds will frighten her."

Albert filled her in on our procedure. "You've got to get people's attention, Ingvild. Smile and be polite, but never shout. We can't force anyone to sign our petitions. If little kids want a free button, give it to them. And if it looks like someone's hanging around just to come on to you, move to another person."

"Come on to me? What's that?"

I explained what Albert meant and Ingvild blushed.

Personally, I think Lexington Avenue attracts lots of people in pushy occupations, who don't like our taking up space outside their favorite store and obstructing the window displays. Albert ignores that stuff but I resent it. I mean, if I'm donating my Saturday, they can at least donate their signature, right?

By two thirty we collected almost a hundred names, over our usual amount. Albert was pleased. "Ingvild seems to be an asset. Maybe people like her accent."

Well, she *did* sound sweet standing there, pleading "Save the little baby seals." Of course, I'd instructed her on who to steer away from. For me, it's a snap to sort out the yuppies from the preppies and the blue-haired ladies in from the suburbs from the street crazies, not to mention the occasional weirdo who wants to stop and talk for *hours.*

Around three o'clock, a real uncooperative type walked by; I can spot them a mile off, so I never bother to give one the pitch. This woman was wearing every variety of living creature—now long dead, of course—thrown on her body. She had a snakeskin bag, a bulky sweater with fur pelts dangling down the sides, bone jewelry, a cowboy hat with feathers in the band, and zebra-skin boots. A mink coat is bad enough, but this woman had half a *zoo* on her back; hardly the type interested in animal rights.

Ingvild dragged her over to our table anyway. She handed her buttons and leaflets and told her about the "little baby seals."

The woman couldn't care less. "I don't think it's fair

for you people to intrude on my day like this. After all, I have rights too. What about my *human* rights?"

I nudged Ingvild. "Skip this one," I whispered. "She probably has a dozen sealskin coats in her closet."

But the woman was hot for an argument. "I should be allowed to wear fur if I like. After all, I pay enough for the privilege."

"And you look disgusting anyway," I muttered. Well I couldn't help it. Selfish, pushy, East Side types always get on my nerves.

"What did you say?" she asked indignantly.

Albert threw me a filthy look. He'd cautioned me dozens of times about being rude. If anyone complained about us, we'd have to leave.

But Ingvild quickly jumped in to smooth things over. "We must protect the rights of baby animals too." Then she began reading aloud from one of our leaflets. "This is what Gandhi said: 'The civilization of a country is judged by the way it treats its animals.' "

The quote didn't carry much weight with this woman. "I don't see what that has to do with anything. Gandhi was an Indian, and in India they have cows wandering all over the streets. Surely that's dreadfully unhealthy. Besides, in India, they probably can't *afford* seal coats."

That's when I joined in. "Look lady, a hundred thousand seals will be slaughtered in Canada and Norway this year. Don't you think that's kind of horrible?"

"Well, it's not *my* fault. Let the Norwegians do something about it!"

"I am Norwegian," said Ingvild, "and I'm *trying* to do something."

Somehow, that argument got her. I guess this spacey

woman figured Ingvild had flown from Norway just to argue with her. She stared blankly for a moment, trying to think up an answer, but she couldn't. "Oh well, in that case," she said, "here's five dollars." She dropped it into the cookie jar and walked away.

Albert was amazed. "Thanks a million, Ingvild. You add credibility to the cause," he said.

That gave him an idea. He began waving petitions, announcing Ingvild had come all the way from Norway to protest the seal slaughters in her country, so the very least people could do would be to come by our table and sign their names.

It worked. By four o'clock, we'd collected another two hundred signatures and sold fifteen dollars worth of buttons.

"You shouldn't have done such a great sales job," I told Ingvild. "Albert will be hounding you to come down every Saturday."

"I don't mind, Jenny."

I didn't mind, either. Ingvild's help had speeded things up, so Albert announced we could leave early and stop for sodas and pizza at a place nearby.

"Pour on that extra cheese," he said, "we're *celebrating!*"

As we waited for our order, Ingvild spoke excitedly about the afternoon's experience. She loved being part of New York crowds and was impressed with Albert's dedication. "I agree with everything in your leaflet."

Personally, I'd never *read* the leaflet.

"You were terrific, Ingvild," he said. "I still can't believe how you turned that woman around. I would've bet she'd never even give us five cents." There was a look of admiration in Albert's eyes I'd never seen there before.

"I did nothing," said Ingvild modestly. "I only spoke to her."

"But you did it so *nicely.* I'm always telling Jenny to do things that way. She has to learn to be more polite to people. With you, it comes naturally, I guess."

Albert smiled. Ingvild smiled back. Suddenly, *I* didn't feel like smiling. Why not? I wondered. After all, I wanted Albert to like Ingvild and Ingvild to like Albert, so why not? I wasn't sure, but I knew I didn't like that twinkle in Albert's eye. It made me feel uneasy.

When our pizza arrived, I dug in. But it didn't taste as good as I'd expected.

Early Sunday morning, Carolyn called collect.

"I know this is expensive, so I won't make a habit of it, but I had to hear your voices and let you know what a marvelous time I'm having here."

Mom got on the phone and Carolyn told her how hard she was working, how friendly everyone was and how they all thought she was a fine student. She'd met lots of people and had already gone skiing.

I said a few words just to seem sociable. Then Carolyn wanted to say hello to Ingvild in Norwegian.

"Your sister learns quickly, Jenny. Her accent is very good. She said my country is cold but my people are warm."

Barfo, right?

"She sounds like a nice person," she added.

Hah!

"Would you like to call home, too?" asked Mom.

Ingvild said she couldn't. Her family lived so far into the woods, they didn't have a phone; that's why she'd promised to write often. Then Mom asked what we had planned for that day so I told her we might go to Columbus Avenue.

Mom has mixed feelings about Columbus Avenue. On one hand, since she'd begun selling West Side real estate she thinks it's great, because Columbus Avenue has gone totally condo and co-op. But personally she doesn't like many aspects of gentrification.

"A woman came into the office yesterday," she explained, "looking for a co-op on Seventy-fourth Street. She asked how long it would take before the neighborhood got rid of all the 'old people with foreign accents' so she could buy in and start knocking down walls. Frankly, I don't think the area can handle another sushi bar. They could use some mom-and-pop stores, but they've all been forced into retirement."

I loved the fact Columbus Avenue had turned into yuppie heaven. It meant lots of new stores and great window-shopping territory for me. But Ingvild agreed with Mom. She thought senior citizens *should* be provided for. She said the Norwegian social system was superior because it did that. Well, the two of them got into a big conversation about "society," which didn't interest me, so I called Liza and invited her to join us later.

Liza was depressed because she'd had another argument with Chuck. "But this one was *serious,* Jen."

"That's what you always say."

"He called me insensitive and pushy. You know I'm the *un*pushiest person in the world."

I didn't say a word.

"Thanks for the moral support, Jen."

"Are you coming or not?"

"Will you stop at the flea market?"

"Sure."

"Then I'm coming."

When I got off the phone, Mom and Ingvild were still talking about socialism. "Thanks for telling me so much about the Norwegian social system," she told Ingvild. "I haven't had such an interesting conversation since Carolyn left."

That comment made me feel sort of rotten. Mom hadn't meant it as an insult to me, but it sounded like one. After all, *we* had conversations, too.

I sensed that annoying shriveling-up feeling in the pit of my stomach, that dreaded sensation I only got when I felt inferior to Carolyn. But Carolyn wasn't around, so what was up? I assumed it was because I'd spoken with her on the phone. Anyway, I ignored it.

"C'mon, Ingvild, let's go to Columbus Avenue."

Ingvild thought we'd taken her to some historic area named after Christopher Columbus, who'd "sailed around the world."

"There's lots of foreign stores," said Liza, "but buying things costs as much as a trip around the world."

Ingvild hadn't bought much since her arrival. "Don't you have money?" I asked.

"Yes, I exchanged my kroner at the bank. But my parents won't be sending much each month, so I must be careful. They said I should look for the riches in the city that don't cost money."

"There aren't any," said Liza.

"I think they meant friendships," she explained.

"Oh," replied Liza. "Sure."

Sometimes, the best part of going to Columbus Avenue is watching *other* people spend money, anyway. They spend it in the outdoor cafés, fancy delis, and sushi bars, buying wine, quiche, Brie, and anything else in fashion. And they spend a fortune in the dreamy shops. There's one called Only Hearts which sells everything with hearts on it—clothing, stationery, underwear. One shop has only Mexican imports, another Peruvian, oh, and dozens more.

And there's definitely no man shortage on Columbus. You can always see some actors—many with parts in soaps, while they wait for their big move to Hollywood prime time—dancers, and other show biz types, all wearing their expensive-but-casual clothes. Young male executives, too —some of those upwardly mobile guys are *hunks.* Last year, when Liza and I were pretending we were primas, we tried bumping into a few, accidentally-on-purpose. Unfortunately, there are tons of gorgeous *girls* around, too, so we didn't have much luck.

The three of us bought chocolate croissants at the bakery, then headed for the outdoor flea market on Seventy-seventh Street. On Sundays vendors set up their concessions in the junior high school playground. There are lots of old and new items, clothing and antiques, all costing less than in stores. It's really a big deal, and vendors come from everywhere to set up on the weekend.

"I found a nice handmade necklace here last time," I told Ingvild, "and this is where Mom does her Christmas shopping."

I didn't mention it was also the place Liza came whenever possible. One particular concession really interested her. It was run by a gorgeous college guy who sold hand-made woolens his parents imported from Britain. Liza always hung around him, pretending she might buy something, while secretly hoping he'd hit on her. He never did, but she never gave up.

"I think I'll check out those sweaters again," said Liza.

Big surprise.

"I'll come, too," said Ingvild, "I like hand-knit things."

I didn't go along. Frankly, I was sick of seeing Liza drool over the guy, so I browsed by the leather belts instead. I found a great white one and asked to have it held until the following week. By then, I'd have my baby-sitting money. I'd be sitting for Jason Petrie, which always paid well.

Then I glanced through old magazines from the forties. Most of the fashions were so old, they were new again. I poked through a bin of antique clothing from the fifties, wishing I could wear that trendy stuff. But I always wind up looking like an orphan or a refugee.

After a while, Liza came hurrying back. "Guess who's in a hot conversation with Mr. Gorgeous who sells the sweaters?"

"Who?"

"Ingvild, naturally. How does that girl do it? She's like a magnet. I've been coming here for ages and I'd never learned his name. Ingvild walked over and learned it in a second. She *asked* him. Hardly the subtle approach, but it worked."

"Well, what is it?"

"Sean. Isn't that marvelous? Sean O'Donnelly. He admired Ingvild's sweater and she told him she'd made it.

Then he said maybe Ingvild could make some just like it for him to sell. Hats and scarves, too, maybe. Sean said she might be able to make lots of money."

"That's great."

"Great? It's fantastic. If only I'd known, I would've learned to knit. I'd make him a sweater for nothing."

"What's so wonderful about this guy?"

"Are you joking? He's a major hunk. If only I'd known he was so heavily into woolens."

We met up with Ingvild a few minutes later. She was flattered by Sean's offer and excited at the prospect of making money, but she wasn't sure she had the time. "Sean gave me his card, but I don't know where this place is."

Eagerly, Liza grabbed the card. "It's called Cable Imports, Incorporated, in Brooklyn Heights. Hey, that's not far—only half an hour on the subway. I could deliver stuff for you. Even better, you could teach me how to knit too. Then we could make things together."

Liza went into a whole number about how she'd always loved handmade woolens—which was news to me—and how she longed to learn to make them herself—another surprise—and how they both should get together and have a knitting party, like Beryl had suggested.

I've always been all thumbs with crafts, so I couldn't get excited about the prospect. But Ingvild thought it was a great idea.

"How about Thursday afternoon?" asked Liza. "I'll come over and you can start giving me lessons."

"Hey, Thursday we always go to the movies together," I reminded her.

"The movie can wait, Jen. This is *important.*"

I was starting to feel left out, so I walked on ahead

and poked through another bin of antique clothing. There was a big sign, EVERYTHING ONE DOLLAR, and I was anxious to find a bargain. There were lots of funky hats and jackets, but they all looked dopey on me. Then Ingvild began rummaging too. She found a pin-striped jacket and an old fedora, and they both looked great on her. She also found a long silk scarf and a wild-looking T-shirt. She'd only spent four dollars, and she looked terrific.

I spent every dime at the discount makeup counter. As I put the cosmetics in my purse, I noticed that peculiar twinge coming back, the shriveling-up feeling that I hated.

What the heck was it? Gas?

I didn't know. I only knew I wasn't in the mood to shop any longer. It was getting late, anyway, and I had to baby-sit for Jason that evening. Ingvild offered to come along so we could do our homework together. Before leaving the flea market, Liza gave Sean one last long, lingering look.

Walking along the avenue, Liza kept pumping Ingvild for more information about Mr. Gorgeous, but Ingvild only said he'd been "sweet." Apparently, Ingvild thought everyone was sweet, including Mr. Greensleeves, one of the neighborhood crazies who skates down the street wearing green rags and shouts at people. Ingvild thought he was a "street performer." We also saw a man with a snake wrapped around his neck and a woman in an evening gown. Columbus Avenue has its share of nutsos, too. Ingvild thought it was like going to the circus. She kept saying how wonderful the city is and how it's filled with so many "amazing sights."

That was ironic, because Ingvild hadn't actually seen the city yet—not the Statue of Liberty, Radio City, Rockefeller Center. Nothing. Only Bloomies, a flea market, and lots of New Yorkers.

"I'll tell you about Jason," I said, ringing the Petrie's doorbell, "so you don't think he's a midget. He's actually a five-year-old genius. He knows all about music, art, math, and science. With a little luck, he might do our homework for us."

"Are you joking?" she asked.

"Just a little. Jason is real smart and he never gives me any trouble about bedtime."

Yeah, Jason is a terrific kid. I'm sure his IQ beats out mine. In fact, he's the only good legacy Carolyn left behind. She'd been his baby-sitter, and so far, Mrs. Petrie was paying me the same rate—double my usual. The Petries are intellectual types, always going off to seminars and things. And Mrs. Petrie doesn't object if I bring a friend along. She says the studious atmosphere is stimulating for Jason.

Jason came running to the door, polite as ever. "Hi, Jenny, who's your friend?"

"This is Ingvild. She's a foreign exchange student from Norway."

"Hi. They exchanged you for Carolyn, right?"

Ingvild smiled. "That's right."

"I like Carolyn. She knows lots of things. Do you know lots of things too?"

"I think so."

"Then I'll probably like you, too. Will you teach me about Norway?"

"If you like."

As I introduced Ingvild to Mrs. Petrie, I could tell she

was figuring out how to turn the evening into a cultural experience for her son. "Welcome, Ingvild. Jason will be listening to music tonight, as usual. If you'd care to tell him some stories about Norway, that would be an added bonus."

Mrs. Petrie left her usual list of emergency numbers and said she'd return at ten. "Tonight, Jason may select a musical piece himself."

After she'd gone, I glanced through the cassettes she'd left on the stereo. I'd hardly call it choosing when everything was classical. I'd never heard the names of most of them.

Ingvild had. "What would you like to hear, Jason? Sibelius is very serious; Tchaikovsky is more fun. My favorite is the Serenade for Strings."

"You like that stuff?" I asked. "What happened to Whitney Houston?"

"I like her, too. I like many kinds of music."

"Oh." I wondered why Ingvild hadn't mentioned that before. I thought we'd discussed *all* the things we liked. Maybe she thought classical music was above my head?

Ingvild put on Tchaikovsky and described its four movements—when the violins come in and junk like that. They were hitting it off well, so I started my homework, which was definitely a disaster area. I'd gotten so behind in math, it was pathetic. After the music lesson, it was time for Jason's snack, which Ingvild offered to get him. When bedtime came around I was still struggling with numbers, so Ingvild offered to read him a story, too.

"Sure," I said, "maybe you should read him *The Snow Queen* again. He likes that one because it's so strange."

After an hour of miserable math, I was still days behind in assignments. They must've been multiplying in my schoolbag. Anyway, before I knew it, Jason came toddling out in his pajamas to say good night—Ingvild had gotten him ready for bed.

"You're going to sleep already? Hey, we haven't even talked tonight."

"That's okay. Me and Ingvild talked. She taught me to say good night in Norwegian."

"That's terrific."

"And she read me *The Snow Queen* in Norwegian, too. It's much stranger that way. I like it even better."

"Then I'll tuck you in now, okay?"

"Never mind. Ingvild will do it."

Ingvild was standing in the doorway, smiling down at Jason as if he were an angel come to life. As she lifted him into her arms, he rubbed his eyes and said, "I like you a lot, Ingvild. You're even nicer than Carolyn."

Watching them leave the room, I realized Jason had never said that to me. He'd *never* said he liked me more than Carolyn—not even when I'd stood on my head to let the blood rush up so he could learn about the workings of the circulatory system. I'd nearly popped a vein for that kid!

When Ingvild returned, I offered her my math answers. "They're probably all wrong, but at least I finished."

"No thanks, Jennifer. I finished also."

"You did? When?"

"Last night."

"Oh. Well then I guess we should start English. Boy, I'm glad we've finally finished with Shakespeare. This play, *A Doll's House,* sounds much easier."

Ingvild said she'd already read the play and it wasn't simple at all. She told me it was a serious social drama about the position of women in society. "If you have trouble with the Norwegian names, I'll help you with the pronunciation."

I felt that twinge again. Only this time, I knew exactly what it was.

Jealousy.

Chapter Eight

All that next week, I got *lots* of twinges. At first I told myself they were symptoms of an allergy attack, a stomach virus, a flu bug—but I knew that wasn't true. It was definitely jealousy.

I was jealous of Ingvild.

And I hated the feeling.

I mean, all my life I'd been comfortable resenting and envying my sister—sometimes even despising her—because I knew she was a lousy person. In spite of all the compliments she received, all the great marks, all the popularity, *I* knew she was rotten. So it was okay.

But Ingvild was *nice,* and sweet and helpful and friendly and intelligent, et cetera, et cetera. Being jealous of a person like that is really *sick,* right?

But I couldn't help it. My grand plan to grow into a new person once Carolyn left had suddenly backfired. I was getting those same old feelings of inferiority I'd had when she was around.

Was I paranoid or what? True, kids at school seemed to like Ingvild. Mom liked her, Liza liked her, Jason liked her, and Albert certainly liked her. And that was okay. But it wasn't okay if they all liked her better than they did me. Was that possible?

I couldn't let anyone suspect I envied Ingvild. I didn't dare mention my feelings to anyone, so I pushed them aside. That wasn't always easy. At times I thought the fates were conspiring to test me.

On Tuesday, Mrs. Petrie called. She said Jason had had a wonderful time being read to in Norwegian. She wanted Ingvild to sit for him again, "so he could benefit from a foreign language." Ingvild invited me along, too, saying we could do our homework together. But it didn't take much brains to realize my best-paying baby-sitting job might be going down the drain.

On Thursday Liza came over, weighted down with bags of wool and ready for her knitting lesson. I had to go to the movies by myself.

On Friday Albert arrived with a pile of animal rights literature for Ingvild. "She's so involved in our cause, I knew she'd want to read this," he said. "Why don't you ever read it, Jenny? It's very interesting."

Even Mom was giving Ingvild special attention. That Sunday she didn't go to the library as usual. Thinking it might help with her dissertation, she stayed home to have a long discussion with Ingvild about the social system in Norway. I didn't bother them. I knew they were busy.

And every day at school kids and teachers stopped to tell me what a great idea it'd been to introduce a foreign exchange student into Emerson.

Ingvild continued getting As and I continued getting Cs.

There were lots of telephone calls for Ingvild: messages about volleyball practice, kids from the study group, things like that. The guidance counselor asked Ingvild to speak to seniors about studying abroad.

Somehow, living with Ingvild had become like living with Carolyn—only worse. I couldn't yell at her, insult her, steal her things or complain about her to my friends—they were all *her* friends now, too. Besides, I didn't want to be angry at her—I *liked* her. That was the most awful part. I hadn't realized I could feel both envy and affection at the same time. It was a schizy feeling!

There was nothing to complain about, anyway. Ingvild was always helpful around the house—cooking, shopping, cleaning, making lunch. But I had to hold myself in every time Mom complimented her on her great meals and terrific study habits. Those compliments annoyed me; each one was like a personal insult hurled in my direction. By some miracle, Ingvild also had time left over to write her parents. Mom'd been nagging me for days to jot off a note to Carolyn, but of course, I hadn't.

"You should become more organized," said Mom. "Make time. Ingvild has study group and volleyball practice, but she still has time to write her parents. Carolyn wants to hear from you. Write and tell her how well you're getting on with Ingvild."

But like I said, I didn't tell anyone *anything.*

The next Saturday, I didn't go to Bloomie's. I told Albert my sinuses were acting up and that I felt miserable.

"That's okay. Ingvild is coming, so don't worry about it."

That comment made me boil!

Before Ingvild left, she gave me her notes on *A Doll's*

House. "You can study them if you like, Jennifer. You need to raise your grade in English."

That comment made me boil too.

Okay, I admit it: when I get depressed, I *wallow* in it. Suddenly my sinuses got worse, along with my ears, eyes, and *teeth*—which reminded Mom it was time for my semi-annual visit to the dentist. She made an appointment for Monday. I argued, saying I hated waiting in Dr. Levine's office for hours, but Ingvild said she'd be happy to keep me company.

"Good," said Mom. "That'll make things much more pleasant, won't it, Jenny?"

"Sure, Mom."

Dr. Levine stared into my mouth in despair. "A cavity. And you haven't been flossing."

For the next hour, over the buzz of the drill excavating a hole down to my toes, I got my semiannual lecture on oral hygiene. When I left the chair, my cheek felt like lead.

"Next time we'll take X rays," said Dr. Levine. "In the meantime, cut out junk foods."

Ingvild was seated in the waiting room. Thinking she was his next patient, Dr. Levine asked her in, so I explained who she was. With a cold professional eye, he glanced directly at her mouth. "You certainly have beautiful teeth, young lady. What country are you from?"

"Norway."

"That explains it. Fish country. I bet you floss too. And you avoid junk foods, right?"

Ingvild nodded.

"I thought so. Take a lesson from your friend, Jennifer. Start caring for your mouth, or you'll have false teeth at forty. See you in six months."

I tried to smile, but only half my face would move.

That night, Liza called.

"I've finished it, Jen—one entire handmade sweater. I thought it'd take ages, but Ingvild's a *terrific* teacher. She's making a sweater, too, and we're both going down to see Sean. You were absolutely right about Ingvild: her coming *was* an omen. If I can get something going with Mr. Gorgeous, I don't care if Chuck ever calls me again. Frankly, I don't think he'll ever make it big in Hollywood."

You get the picture. I was sharing my room with a friendly, helpful, intelligent, studious, generous, socially dedicated person, who *flossed*—a thing I wouldn't wish on my worst enemy.

Psychologically speaking, I'd sunk to a new low. And then I sunk lower: I began wishing *Carolyn* would return. I mean, a good, healthy, low-down, sibling argument would've let off lots of steam. Instead, I continued to grin and bear it.

I'd made a promise to myself and I'd keep it. After all, Ingvild couldn't help being perfect, right? It was her nature, just as mine was to be argumentative, unscholarly, and moody. Schoolwork came easy to Ingvild and friendships even easier. I guess there are some people in the world on whom the sun always shines—which, of course, leaves others of us in the shadows.

After all, I'd wanted change and I'd gotten it. Right?

It wasn't for the better, but sometimes the fates play dirty tricks like that.

Chapter Nine

There was a major change at school, too. Downstairs, a giant leak burst the plumbing. The cafeteria and auditorium walls had to be ripped out so all the old pipes could be replaced. That made both facilities off-limits indefinitely. I hoped that meant shorter school days, since we'd have no place to eat lunch or have assembly. But the principal had other ideas.

Mr. Corbett made the announcement over the loudspeaker (our PA system is the pits, so it sounded like his voice was coming from Mars instead of his office):

"Every effort will be made not to disrupt your academic schedules. The faculty of Fordham University, several blocks away, has kindly offered to accomodate our students during the interim. They have a large cafeteria, more than adequate for our needs. Needless to say, all Emerson students will be expected to behave in a respectable manner while on their premises. I'm initiating several scattered lunch schedules until this temporary inconvenience is over."

Leaving Ptomaine City behind even briefly would improve my day. It was also a good excuse to tell Ingvild not to bring homemade lunches—not that they weren't good. They were terrific. Her brown-bag specials had become the social event of our lunch table. Vivian loved seeing what new tasty morsels Ingvild had come up with: carrot curls, fresh fruit salads, fancy little sandwiches. Once she'd even brought homemade bread. I'd already concluded Ingvild's day had several extra hours. Anyway, the kids couldn't wait to see what Ingvild would make for us next. Whenever she made vegetable salad, she'd bring extra for Albert, knowing he was a vegetarian. Guys are suckers for stuff like that, which proves how very unliberated they are.

As we walked to Fordham during lunch period, Liza insisted we be alone, so we hung back from the group.

"What's up?" I asked.

"We went to see Sean yesterday. Didn't Ingvild tell you?"

"No, I went to bed real early last night and she hadn't come in yet. How'd it go? Did he like the sweaters? More important, did he like *you?*"

"He didn't look at me *or* the sweater. I wore my fingers to the bone knitting and purling, for absolutely nothing. Sean O'Donnelly is a major creep, Jen; I'm talking *major.* Turns out his family employs an entire village in Ireland to make hand-knit items, so he certainly didn't need ours. That guy wasn't interested in *woolens,* after all."

"Then why'd he give Ingvild his card?"

"Ulterior motives."

"Such as?"

"Such as hitting on her, that's such as. That was his plan, see: get Ingvild to come to his place in Brooklyn—

which, by the way, isn't a store at all but his home address. He lives there alone; his folks are in Europe. To make a gruesome story short, he has the hots for Ingvild. Luckily, *I* was there to mess up his sordid scheme. There I was, standing like a dope with a hand-knit reindeer sweater. Know how hard it is to knit reindeers into a sweater, Jen? It's almost impossible. And there he was, ignoring the fact I existed while he made his play for Ingvild."

"No kidding? What'd she do?"

"Well, she said he should call her up sometime. But I think you should fill her in on guys like that. After all, you're her best friend here, so it's your responsibility. I'm telling you, that guy is a deceitful phony—pretending he was interested in knitted goods. Can you beat it? I certainly wouldn't want a dear friend of mine involved with him. Anyway, now I'm stuck with that sweater, which took me days to make, and in which I look like a travel poster. All things considered, you should have a heart-to-heart with Ingvild. Scare her off this guy. She's too sweet and innocent to get mixed up with an operator like that. Don't you agree?" We continued down the street in silence for a minute. "Jen, I'm baring my soul here, don't you have anything to say?"

What could I say? It sounded like Ingvild had struck it rich. With her luck, she'd probably wind up Mrs. Cable Imports, Inc. What was her magic power, anyhow? But I couldn't break the promise to myself, so I kept quiet about my feelings.

Fordham University's cafeteria is fabulous. It's on an upper floor, large and airy, with windows that look out over the street and a little terrace area—a vast improvement over Ptomaine City at Emerson. The hot lunch counter had a great selection. But the best part of the deal were all the college students gathered there—college *guys,* I should say. Not one of them was slamming sandwiches against the wall or making tuna fish ooze from his mouth like the jerks at Emerson. The sight of so many guys over the age of eighteen gave my heart a lift.

"If I'd known we were going to heaven," sighed Liza, "I would've worn new jeans."

I noticed two handsome guys seated together at a corner table. Liza spotted them, too. "Let's sit *there.* With any luck, one of them will notice us. I'll mind the seats while you get on line, okay? Buy me a Coke and a burger, and I'll pay you back."

I was glad our lunch group had been temporarily disbanded. Lately, Albert and Ingvild only talked about social issues. Ingvild had already taken a seat on the other side of the cafeteria, next to the Terrible Three. I'd noticed she'd suddenly begun spending lots of time with them, but I couldn't figure out why. Ingvild waved in my direction, but I pretended not to notice. I'd rather die than sit with the ditzies.

I bought lunch, then returned to the other table. Liza kept trying to get the attention of at least one of the guys, but they both had their heads buried in books. Figuring them for brainy types, she made some casual references to the Ibsen play we were studying in English.

"Tell me, Jennifer, what do you think of that guy Torvald? I think he's dreadfully narrow-minded, don't you agree? If I'd been Nora, I would've dumped him immediately, wouldn't you?"

"Huh? Oh, yeah."

"Of course, I think Nora is too frivolous to be considered a true tragic heroine, don't you agree?"

"Right."

Unfortunately, there was no response from the guys. They began shoveling down their salads.

After we'd eaten, Ingvild stopped by our table to tell me she'd be home late. "I have volleyball practice. I'll be playing my first game next weekend."

"You still enjoy playing?" asked Liza in disbelief.

"It's very good exercise. Of course, at home I'd be skiing already. There's much snow in Norway now. In Holmenkollen, there is snow in October."

The two guys, who hadn't even *glanced* at us, suddenly came to life. They brightened up as soon as Ingvild began talking.

"You've been to *Holmenkollen?*" one asked excitedly.

Ingvild was surprised. "Yes. You know this place?"

"Naturally," said the other. "Holmenkollen has the best winter sports events in Norway. Have you skied there?"

"Oh yes."

So the guys were ski buffs—just our luck. Me and Liza knew zip about skiing and cared even less. But it didn't take long before they were both in a hot conversation with Ingvild.

At first, I thought they were all speaking Norwegian, but then I realized it was ski language. They talked about the stem christie, sitzmarks, moguls, and the wedeln. The only ski term I knew was snow bunny, so I kept my mouth shut.

Me and Liza stared at one another as the guys introduced themselves to Ingvild. They were Patrick and Ron, both phys ed majors, proud of the fact they'd skied the best slopes in Europe during winter school breaks.

"I hope ski conditions will be good upstate soon," said Patrick, "but we can't always get up to Hunter, Windham, or Big Vanilla. How long have you been skiing, Ingvild?"

"Since I am three. In the city, I miss the slopes."

"Then go to Van Cortland Park," said Ron. "That's nearby."

"Really?" asked Ingvild. "It's possible to ski in the *city*?"

"Sure," he explained. "As soon as it snows, we go up every Sunday. Only cross-country, of course. There's no deep powder, so naturally you can't slalom, but it's not bad."

Liza nudged me. "I can't believe this," she muttered. "We couldn't get to first base, but these guys are falling all over Ingvild."

I couldn't admit what I really thought, so I lied. "That's great—I guess. Don't you think so?"

Liza thought a minute. "Yeah, I suppose. Sure, I guess it's great to have a friend with magnetism. If we stick close enough, some of it will probably rub off."

As we walked back to school, Liza put her arm around Ingvild and casually mentioned she'd love to learn more about skiing. "It's something I've always wanted to do, but I've never had the time. Maybe you could teach me soon, okay?"

To me, skiing seemed more impossible than knitting, so I walked along behind, feeling totally out of things.

Chapter Ten

The following week, Liza announced she was throwing a sleep-over party on Saturday night. She invited me, Beryl, and Ingvild. If Liza was having a party, it meant she hadn't patched up her argument with Chuck. Saturday nights were always reserved for him.

Anyway, I began looking forward to it. A few days of schlumping around was my limit, so I made a momentous decision. If Carolyn had been around, she would've put some fancy psychological label on it. She might've said I'd come to a crossroads of maturity or something. For once, she might've been right.

I'd decided I wouldn't lay down and die just because Ingvild was popular. I mean, it didn't make me less a person, right? Okay, so Ingvild was better in school, but that didn't make me zero, right?

Right! I secretly began a campaign to upgrade my self-image. I began thinking about that Lovey Face contest. Beryl was right: self-confidence *was* the key to success, so winning at that audition would really boost my ego—not to mention my bank account, probably. But getting better grades would help, too, so I began to make a real academic effort.

During study period, I began helping out in the school office, for extra credits toward my midterm mark. And I promised myself I'd hand in a *decent* English project.

We continued having lunch at Fordham, which was a terrific deal. The food was always great and me and Liza always grabbed seats next to the gorgeous jocks. They never said anything, but at least they smiled occasionally.

During baby-sitting jobs, I'd make sure I was all caught up on homework.

Ingvild was spending more of her time at volleyball practice and the library. She'd also started traveling around the city by herself. Being away from her helped my jealousy subside; that nagging feeling inside was leaving and I was glad to see it go. I was even glad to be working on my English project.

We'd been asked to compare the characters in *A Doll's House* to a modern couple, then draw conclusions. I wrote that a marriage like the one Nora had in the play couldn't exist today, because women aren't considered dolls any longer. We're all out in the world fighting for survival, just like men. I tied up my theme with the women's lib movement. I wrote six pages, which were pretty good, I thought. When I'd finished, I told myself if I received a decent grade, I'd never be jealous of anyone again, that the fates weren't really against me—all kinds of psych-yourself-up stuff like that.

On Friday Mr. Freeman read the best papers aloud to the class. First he read Ingvild's. She'd written that Nora's constant lying in the play was actually a poetic example of the great lie representing her entire life. She'd mentioned women's lib, too, but said there were still lots of marriages like Nora's, where women are subservient, and that's why the play's theme is still relevant.

It was a good essay. Freeman gave her an A and congratulated her on her insights into a complex character.

He read three other papers, then handed them all back. I held my breath, waiting to see my mark. I put my hand over the paper, slowly removing one finger at a time until the grade was visible. It was a B plus—the best grade I'd ever gotten on an English paper in my life!

I nearly told Freeman he must've made a mistake, but when he stopped to compliment me on my improved work, I knew I'd earned it.

At last, an ego booster. It felt great!

On Saturday Albert took the bus to Washington with an animal rights group, to picket outside the White House. I didn't go along. Instead, I spent the afternoon packing my bag to bring to Liza's house. True, it was only two blocks away and I was only staying overnight, but we always packed for sleep-overs. We'd bring all our makeup, new clothes, and shampoo and curlers and have a cosmetic-fashion pig out before going out to dinner. It would be even more fun than usual because Beryl was bringing tons of sample make up and freebie fashions she'd received modeling.

Ingvild couldn't believe all the junk I was packing. "I didn't bring that much from Norway," she joked.

"This'll be a good time for you to experiment with makeup. Beryl is bringing a storefull too."

I was really feeling up. My good English grade had dragged me out of the psychological dumps. To me it was a sign I could look jealousy in the face and beat it.

I thought of the Lovey Face contest again. If I could improve in English, I could do *anything*.

At four o'clock, we all met at Liza's house.

"My parents have left," she told us. "They knew they'd never get into the bathroom."

Our sleep-over bashes were always dreaded by Liza's parents. Once it'd taken Mrs. Shapiro a week to scrape off the mudpack splatters we'd accidentally gotten on her bathroom walls.

When I saw the amount of stuff Beryl was unloading, I knew Mrs. Shapiro's bathroom would soon need a major industrial cleanup. She'd brought cosmetics for our nails, hair, toes, and elbows—not to mention herbal cleansers and a face scrub made from crushed apricot pits.

"We should've started at noon," I said. "Can we make a dent in this stuff before dinner?"

"Personally," said Liza, "I plan to try everything. I'm desperately in need of a new look. My face has gone sour on me."

"I've just the thing," said Beryl. "Try this collagen skin mask. It rips off dead cells, just like peeling a grape. Try the leg-waxing cream too. It gets to the root of the hair, underneath the surface. No girl can feel good about herself when she has stubble."

Liza grabbed all the hair-removal products. "That's my problem area."

As I sorted through the cosmetics I casually brought up the Lovey Face contest. "Have you heard any more details?"

"I think they're interested in fair-skinned types with a fresh, natural, outdoorsy look. Let's experiment making you look natural, Jenny. A made-up effect is easy, but natural takes much longer. You'll have to put on makeup, rub it off, then reapply more. Continue doing that until it looks like Mother Nature's idea."

Beryl gave me a ton of stuff to try. Ingvild experimented, too, but she couldn't apply makeup. The mascara collected in globs on her eyelashes and she overshot her lip line. When she'd finished, we laughed at the results.

"You need lots more lessons," said Beryl, "but you'll get the hang of it."

As Liza let her collagen mask set she griped about Chuck. "That worm hasn't called me in days. He said he's preparing for a big audition, but I don't believe it. Don't you hate guys who hate liberated women and call them pushy? What do they want from us, anyway? I mean, they take our hair spray, our purses, and our mousse—then complain we're not feminine enough."

Beryl agreed. "Maybe they don't know what they want. I think it's like that Ibsen play we just read in class."

"Don't mention English," said Liza. "I refuse to discuss Freeman's prejudicial grading system."

That was odd, because Liza was usually anxious to brag about her English marks.

"Why don't you call Chuck?" asked Ingvild. "Must you wait for him to call?"

"Sure, I could call. Naturally. But I don't want to give him the satisfaction, you know? If only I had some good excuse, some legitimate reason that has nothing to do with our relationship."

"Tell him there's a bomb set to go off in his lobby," I suggested.

"Tell him there's a good part opening in a soap," said Beryl.

"Tell him *I'd* like to meet him," added Ingvild. "I haven't met anyone in show business since I've been here."

"Hey, that's not a bad idea," agreed Beryl. "Appeal to his male ego. He has one, doesn't he?"

"Are you serious?" asked Liza. "He has an ego big enough for three guys. Chuck says ego is more important than talent if you want to make it in show business."

"Then he'll probably come running," said Beryl. "Tell Chuck to meet us at Charlie's because someone wants to hear all about his career."

Liza agonized over that idea for half an hour before she finally called. "He'll be there at six," she said, pleased and relieved. Then she realized she hadn't peeled off her face mask and went running toward the bathroom.

"I'd better help her," sighed Beryl. "She's still an amateur."

I kept applying makeup, rubbing it off, and reapplying it—achieving the "natural" look was very time-consuming. Ingvild kept testing more cosmetics, getting more unnatural-looking by the minute. I admit to a degree of pleasure at finding something I actually did *better*. I felt my chances of winning Lovey Face getting closer.

When we'd finally exhausted our faces, Beryl unpacked the designer samples she'd brought. "I warn you, they're awfully trendy. But fashion should be startling, don't you think?"

She unloaded belts, fishnets, puffy blouses, gauzy slacks. "Poke through them and come up with something that makes a bold fashion statement."

I chose slacks with dozens of zippered pockets and an oversize striped shirt.

"Don't wear it *that* way," she said, tying it up on either side.

"You sure I don't look like a laundry bag?"

"It's the only way to wear it!"

Liza found a miniskirt and a neon sweatshirt splattered with painted graffiti.

"That's right, be *daring*," said Beryl.

Ingvild tried on things, too, but kept making faces. Before we left for Charlie's she went into the bathroom; when she came out, she'd changed back into her own clothes, rinsed her hair, and washed off all the makeup.

Beryl was disgusted. "You've thrown our entire experiment down the drain."

"I feel better this way," Ingvild explained. "You girls look fine with all these things, but I don't."

Beryl stared at Ingvild with a professional eye. "Maybe you're right. Your original look is the true you, and finding your look is essential. Yes, it's inspired. Who would've thought of achieving that freshscrubbed natural look by being absolutely *natural.*" She glanced over at me. "You know, Jenny, I think Ingvild should try out for that Lovey Face contract, too."

My stomach tightened into a knot. Lovey Face was *mine.* Sure, I'd have to compete with other girls—but not Ingvild.

"Oh no," said Ingvild awkwardly. "Jenny is going to try out for that."

"Well, what's wrong with *both* of you trying out?" Beryl insisted. "It's a very democratic contest."

I could've killed Beryl right then. Didn't she know I'd

been looking forward to this, planning for it, praying I'd win? Well, maybe she didn't, but she could've kept her mouth shut anyway. I mean, she'd put me in a totally rotten position. If I appeared offended, I'd look like a selfish pig; so I didn't say a word. I felt all the gains I'd made quickly slipping away. My chances of winning Lovey Face were slipping away as well.

I considered the evening ruined. I suddenly felt like a fool in all those trendy clothes (I *did* look like a laundry bag). I longed to slip back into my jeans too. But that would've drawn attention to the whole rotten deal. Plus, I was furious at Liza for not even *noticing* how I felt. She was too busy preparing for her encounter with Chuck, coaching Ingvild in what to say.

"Ask Chuck about his parts on Broadway. After a while, I'll step into the conversation, and before you know it, everything will be back to normal again."

For a second, I had a mad impulse to drag Liza from the room and tell her I couldn't stand holding in my resentment toward Ingvild another second. But I didn't. Instead, we all left for Charlie's Ice Cream Parlor.

Chapter Eleven

When we arrived, Chuck was seated at a corner table, glancing at himself in the mirror. Liza introduced Ingvild, then nudged her into action as we all ordered burgers.

"Are you really an actor?" she asked. "I've never met an actor before."

"Well you're meeting one now," he said proudly. "Six soaps, three Broadway shows, and a possible prime time special this spring."

You could stick Chuck's entire career on the head of a pin, but he made it sound terrific. Ingvild seemed very interested. Chuck seemed equally interested in her, especially when he learned she was from Norway.

"I'd like to study your accent," he said. "I can do Irish, English, and Italian, but Scandinavian is tough. A guy has to diversify if he wants to make it big, so accents are important."

Liza thought things were going well. Chuck had already forgotten he was supposed to still be mad at her. He was too busy telling us all about his Off Broadway audition coming up.

"I'm supposed to play a termite. It's real heavy symbolic stuff."

"Oh, I'm sure," said Liza.

"You bet," he added. "That guy who won the Oscar for *Amadeus* once played leaves in a Fruit of the Loom commercial, so you never know."

Ingvild agreed. "Tell me more about the plays you've been in."

As if he needed to be asked! For the next ten minutes, he reeled off his credits. Beryl spied some friends at another table and made a quick getaway, but Ingvild kept listening. When our burgers arrived, Chuck invited her to his upcoming audition.

"Liza thinks stuff like that is dull, but I can tell you're different. You appreciate theater, don't you?"

"Oh yes. In Norway, the theater is . . . What's that word?"

"You mean subsidized?" he asked.

"That's right. Actors make a good living."

Chuck nodded. "Sounds like a civilized country. We should have that here, too. What's the good of a union if there aren't any jobs? You Norwegians know how to treat artists—with *respect.*"

"I also have acted," said Ingvild. "Only in school plays, but I very much enjoyed it. Acting is very important."

Chuck leaned in closer. "Listen, could you teach me that terrific accent of yours?"

Ingvild blushed. "All right. If you like, I'll try."

"Great. We'll get together real soon. Say, maybe you'd like to see my glossies?"

"Your what?"

"My photos; all actors have photos. Mine are really great."

Liza bit into her burger so hard, she squirted ketchup all over her neon sweatshirt. "Look at that," she squealed, staring at the red splotch mixing in with the graffiti splatters. "I hope I haven't ruined it."

"How can you tell?" joked Chuck. "Where'd you get that wacky outfit, anyway? Are you planning to see *The Rocky Horror Show* tonight?"

Liza clamped down on my arm. "Jen, could you come into the bathroom and help me wash this off? Excuse us."

"Take your time," said Chuck. "I haven't told Ingvild half my credits yet."

Liza's face was beet red when we got to the ladies' room. She quickly latched the door. "Never mind the shirt, Jen, I've got to *talk* to you. I don't like the way things are going out there."

"But this whole thing was—"

"I know what you're going to say: this meeting was my idea. Maybe it was, but Chuck seems entirely too interested in Ingvild—*entirely*. Did you hear him offer to show her his glossies? What a come-on! That's the same line he used on *me*. And he invited her to his audition. *I* always go to those, no matter how boring. He's definitely making a play for her."

"But she—"

"Sure, I know you think Ingvild is perfectly wonderful, and that's why I didn't say anything about those other incidents, but—"

"What other incidents?"

"Sean, for one thing. That girl *stole* him right out from under me, but I didn't say a word—because I know she's your friend, your foreign exchange buddy, your roommate, your *omen*. So I kept my mouth shut. And I didn't mention our English assignment, either. I really boiled when Freeman read her paper aloud. He never even mentioned mine, which was just as good. I'm a terrific English student, but he only gave me a B minus. I'll bet Freeman is giving Ingvild preferential treatment. Anyway, I overlooked it. I even invited her to my sleep-over, not to be petty. But I was boiling inside, believe me."

"Liza, if you'd only—"

"I know what you're going to say, Jen. If only I could be more philosophical about things. But I *can't.* I know Ingvild is sweet and wonderful and all that garbage, but I don't care. Look at the way she attracted those college guys. It's not *fair.* Okay, she has magnetism, but she's not pulling Chuck away from me. I know you'll think I'm terrible but I'm coming right out with this: I'm *jealous* of that girl!"

A tremendous weight suddenly lifted from me. Hearing Liza express all my own feelings and resentments was wonderful, and I couldn't help laughing. "Really, Liza. You're jealous of Ingvild?"

"Thanks a heap for the sympathy, Jen. Yes, I'm jealous—*insanely.*"

"But—"

"No, Jen, don't tell me she's really a great person; I know that. That's why I feel so rotten. All those fantastic lunches she drags into school. She's *nice* to everybody, too. But I don't care if you think I'm a beast, I can't help it. Suddenly, I can't *stand* Ingvild. Isn't that awful?"

"No, it's *wonderful,*" I said with relief, "because I thought I was the only one. I'm just as jealous of her as you are!"

"*You?* Well, why didn't you say something?"

"I couldn't." All my hidden feelings came pouring out as I went through my whole list of grievances: how Ingvild (unintentionally, of course) had taken away my best baby-sitting job; how she'd impressed Albert *and* Mom—not to mention my *dentist.* "But worst of all, I'm afraid she's ruined my chances to win that Lovey Face contract."

"How? When did that happen?"

"At your house, stupid. Beryl said Ingvild should try out too. She's far more natural and fresh-scrubbed so you know what that means."

"Sure. With her luck, she'll probably win."

"Naturally. I mean, it took me two hours to look the way she does after she *washes her face.* It's really been rough, Liza. I thought improving my grades would help me resent her less, but if she takes Lovey Face away from me . . ."

"Jen, you should've told me all this *instantly.*"

"I would've, but you were too preoccupied trying to maneuver Chuck."

"*That* worm. I'm sorry, Jen. I'd no idea you felt the same way about Ingvild. In fact, I thought you were beginning to like her better than *me.*"

"And I thought the same about you. All that knitting and skiing stuff."

"But that was to attract *guys.*" Liza sighed. "Well what should we do about this mess?"

"What *can* we do? Nothing. After all, Ingvild didn't set out to mess things up. I think it's some awful by-product of all her niceness."

By now, Liza's stain had slowly begun drying into her sweatshirt, so she began washing it off. "Well, if *you're* jealous and *I'm* jealous, we should combine our jealousy and turn it into—something."

"Okay. Have you read a book that would give us a clue as to what?"

"Not this time."

"Then we'll have to grin and bear it," I said.

"Think there's any chance Ingvild might suddenly become *rotten?* Then we could tell her off."

"Hardly. Ingvild isn't going to change."

"Then maybe *we* should, Jen. If Ingvild won't change, maybe we can."

"Like how, exactly?"

"Look, I just came up with the idea. Give me time."

Someone started banging on the bathroom door. "Who fell in the toilet?"

Liza quickly finished washing up. When we returned to our table, Chuck was delivering the famous Garbo line, "I want to be alone," in a feeble Norwegian accent.

Ingvild laughed. "That doesn't sound right," she said. "But I'll help you work on it."

"Chuck didn't even notice I was gone," muttered Liza. "He's worse than a worm, he's an *amoeba*."

"Is everyone having fun?" asked Beryl, smiling brightly as she returned to our table.

"Heaps," mumbled Liza, and slipped into icy silence.

I hoped she was thinking up a solution to our mutual problem. Even if there was none, I felt much better knowing she knew that I knew that we both felt the same way.

As we sipped our sodas, Ingvild noticed the atmosphere had changed. "Is everything all right? she whispered. "Will Liza and Chuck be friends again now?"

"Sure," I said. "Everything is great now, Ingvild. Thanks a lot."

"Don't you just love sleep-over dates?" said Beryl, oblivious to everything that was happening. "What shall we do next?"

"I haven't finished telling Ingvild about my career yet," said Chuck. "She wants to hear everything—don't you, Ingvild?"

Ingvild smiled and nodded.

Liza smiled too. Then through clenched teeth she muttered, "We'd better think of something, Jen—and *fast.*"

Chapter Twelve

On Monday, Ingvild went to study group, which meant she wouldn't be home until nine. Liza came over at six to have a "serious conference" regarding our problem.

"Why do I feel guilty about this?" I asked uneasily.

"Search me. We're not attacking Ingvild, we're attacking our problem, which just happens to *be* Ingvild."

"But *how* can we attack it?"

"Analytically, that's the only way. We'll catalogue our assets, then Ingvild's; then we'll know what we're lacking."

"Don't bother—the answer is *everything.*"

"We'll treat this like a math equation. What particular qualities does Albert like about Ingvild?"

"He says she's nice to strangers. And she reads all his animal rights literature."

Liza nodded as she started taking notes. "See, we're making progress already. Could you try being nice for a change?"

"What?"

"Well, extra nice, I mean. Read those leaflets. Then be super polite when you hand them out to people."

"I can manage that, but Albert is also thrilled about those incredible salads Ingvild brings to school."

"Well you can scrape carrots, too, can't you? And read some books about animals or vegetarians or something; that'll impress him. As for me, I know what attracts Chuck. He feels he's found a kindred spirit because Ingvild is so interested in acting. So I thought I'd try out for the school drama club."

"Good. That would revive his interest."

"As for the world in general, I think the guys like Ingvild because she's interested in sports. Do you think we could bring ourselves to—"

"No *way,* Liza. I'm not trying out for the volleyball team!"

"I was merely going to suggest we go see a few games."

"Oh. Okay. What else?"

"Wanna try baking bread? She's good at that too."

"Okay," I agreed.

"But not knitting; I've already struck out there."

"Well, Ingvild sews, too. She got lots of compliments on those slacks she made last week."

"Right. We'll pick up some patterns and give that a shot. What else?"

"Is this a five-year plan? Already I'll have to read and scrape and sew, go to sappy games, plus be charming all the time. Isn't that enough for starters?"

"Okay, I guess. Just one more thing. When you wake up in the morning, say to yourself, 'Every day in every way, I'm getting better and better.' I read that in a book, so I started saying it this morning. Visualization is another good tool. Visualize who you want to be and it helps you *become* that person."

"Really? Does that stuff work?"

"Who knows? When Albert and Chuck start drooling over us again, that's when we'll know."

The next day after school, our master strategy began. Me and Liza went to the library and dragged home tons of books. Hers were on the theater, mine were about animals and vegetarians. We also picked up two simple patterns and some fabric at Woolworth.

"It only took Ingvild an hour to make her slacks," I said, "so let's try it tonight."

"Sure. We can use your mom's sewing machine, if Ingvild doesn't catch on."

"She's with her study group again. They're working on an extra-credit project in French."

"Translating all of French literature, no doubt. Say Jen, why don't we crash that study group? There's probably at least one passable-looking guy in it."

"Let's make slacks first. I'm not ready to compete with superbrains."

Whoever named those patterns Simplicity has a truly warped sense of humor. Liza and I spent an hour figuring out how to read the stupid thing, after which we spent another hour laying out the pieces on the rug. Then we cut, pinned, clipped curves, and matched seams and notches for another hour before we could actually start using the machine—which had no thread in it, and we took forever figuring out how to thread the bobbin. Our "simple" drawstring slacks were turning into a lifetime project.

And mine soon turned into a major disaster when I suddenly realized I'd sewn the pieces together *backwards.*

"You think I could wear these inside-out?" I asked, modeling them.

Liza frowned. "That depends. Do you want compliments or insults?"

I glanced at the slacks in the mirror. The ankles were too tight, the waist too big, and all the seams were showing. I ripped out all the stitches and began again.

We'd also managed to turn the living room into a shambles. (I hoped Mom wouldn't notice the place where I'd cut her tablecloth!)

When Ingvild came home, naturally she wondered what was going on. "What are you making?"

Liza held up her slacks, which looked as pathetic as mine. "Dishrags, I guess," she mumbled. "I mean, *pajamas.*"

"Just the bottoms," I added, "we'll do the tops another day."

We quickly cleaned up the mess, then threw all the fabric in the rag bin underneath the sink.

Strike one!

On Wednesday night when Albert called, I was prepared.

"I didn't see you after school today," he said.

"No, I rushed home to bake some bread."

"To what?"

"Bake bread. It's a relaxing hobby. I'll bring you some on Saturday. I thought we'd hand it out to all those *dear, sweet* people who sign our petitions. Won't that be *nice,* Albert?" I must've sounded like a sap.

"Sure, I guess it would be, but I'm not going Saturday. Ingvild is playing in her first game against Franklin High. I promised I'd be there."

"Then I'll be there, too. I *love* volleyball."

"Have you been okay lately, Jen? I get the feeling something odd is going on."

"Don't be silly. I'll see you at the game."

I hung up and returned to my baking. Thank goodness I wouldn't need any bread for Saturday. Only one loaf turned out, and it looked like a small gray lump.

Strike two, I guess.

I wondered if Liza was doing any better. Over lunch at Fordham the next day, I asked how her drama club plans were working out.

"I tried out and got a part in next month's play."

"Terrific."

"Not quite. The minute I got in, I called Chuck to brag about it, hoping that would impress him. So now he's coming to see the show."

"What's the problem?"

"I just received my part. They're doing *Our Town,* and I was cast as one of the dead people seated in the cemetery. I'm stuck with rehearsals twice a week and I have *no lines.* Hardly an impressive dramatic debut."

"Strike three," I grumbled.

"What's that mean?"

"Maybe we should stop trying to compete with Ingvild."

"Are you *serious?* I haven't even *begun.*"

"But it's pointless, Liza. Life is easier for some people.

Doing well and impressing everyone comes naturally to Ingvild, like her blond hair and terrific skin."

"No. We're not giving up. We'll prove to ourselves we're just as good as she is or . . ."

"Or what?"

"Who knows? Maybe we can ship her off to a *Friday the Thirteenth* camp."

We glanced over at Ingvild, who was having lunch with the Terrible Three again.

"What does she *see* in those jerks?" asked Liza.

"Ingvild says they're actually okay. She thinks they act weird because they're shy."

"Shy? They're *jerks*. Acting weird is inevitable."

I felt that if we continued running around trying to keep up with Ingvild, we'd look like even bigger jerks. That was inevitable too.

Then came Saturday and the big volleyball game. Albert, Liza, and I went together and got good seats up front. I pretended to love the shouting and distinct aroma of perspiration filling the gym.

After an hour, Emerson and Franklin were tied and the girls on the Franklin team were out for blood. Franklin has a real strong team, which usually beats every other school. The score was tied at fourteen, so it was touch and go. The first team to score the next two consecutive points would win.

Ingvild—looking great on the court, blond hair flying, et cetera—hit a powerful serve over the net. Franklin missed it. She served again. They missed again. She'd broken the tie and won the game for Emerson!

The kids went wild. Dozens ran out on the court to

congratulate her—including Albert. I started to run out, too, but Liza wouldn't budge.

"C'mon," I coaxed.

"No."

"Look, I thought we were supposed to become sports enthusiasts. After all, Ingvild won for our school, right?"

Liza slammed her feet into the bench and clamped her arms around her chest. "There's another, more *important* competition going on here, Jen, and *I* want to score the winning point."

Honestly, she was beginning to sound like a real spoiled brat. "I'm going," I said. "Sulk, if you like."

"Two words will make you change your mind, Jen. *Lovey Face.* You'll never win that contract until you gain some confidence. And you'll never do *that* until we do something better than *she* does."

"Okay," I agreed reluctantly, "what'll we try next?"

"Every day, in every way, I'm getting better and better." That's what I told myself each morning when I woke up. But as the weeks went by, I found that harder and harder to believe.

Things went along as usual at home. Mom was absolutely thrilled that Ingvild was getting along so wonderfully. Carolyn kept sending ten-page letters from Norway, saying she was getting along wonderfully, too.

But *I* wasn't. All my life had been spent competing against Carolyn, without success, and now I was doing the same with Ingvild—so far, equally unsuccessfully. We'd still do our homework together sometimes, go shopping together, even go sightseeing together; but things just weren't the same anymore.

Liza kept telling me I was stupid to feel so rotten when we were only trying to improve ourselves. "Listen," she reasoned, "when Chuck goes up for a part, he tries to beat out everyone else by being the best, right? There's nothing wrong with that, so what's the big deal here?"

Maybe she was right.

The next step in Liza's strategy was for us to make some points with the two gorgeous jocks from Fordham. But that plan ended before it began. Mr. Corbett made a "grave announcement" over the loudspeaker one Monday morning:

"I'm sorry to inform you all, despite the fact that repairs in the cafeteria are still incomplete, our students can no longer use the Fordham facilities. Last Friday, a small group of Emerson girls vandalized the bar area, removing several bottles of alcohol. Their identities are as yet unknown, but we urge these misguided students to come forward immediately and admit their offense. In any event, a full investigation is underway, so all those involved will eventually be held accountable. For the interim, lunch periods will be spent in your respective homerooms. I regret that such a small group has seen fit to inconvenience all the rest of you."

Everyone whispered and wondered who the unknown "misguided" students might be. But if anyone had a clue, they weren't telling.

Anyway, with Fordham off-limits, it was back to homemade lunches. I used the opportunity to make Albert one of those vegetarian salads Ingvild usually prepared. Since I can barely chew early in the morning, it wasn't easy. I chopped veggies, then dumped them all in a plastic container. That afternoon, when my eyes were fully open and Albert began eating it, I realized I hadn't done such a great job.

"How's it taste?" I asked.

Albert tried covering up an extremely pained expression with an unconvincing grin. "A little gritty, and maybe a little sandy, but *terrific,*" he choked.

Okay, so maybe I'd forgotten to scrape the carrots. And wash the lettuce. And I might've forgotten to pull the strings off the celery, too. But it's the thought that counts.

If I were still counting, that probably would've been strike ten.

But as long as Liza was undaunted, I had to be, too. Since Chuck was coming to see the play, she kept trying to convince Mrs. Westheimer, the drama teacher, to expand her part to include at least a *few* lines. But Mrs. Westheimer was also undaunted. "Liza, you are merely one of the unnamed, unspecified, *unspoken* dead," she explained. "If Thorton Wilder had wished otherwise, he would have specifically noted that in the text."

The evening of the play Liza was still trying to figure out a way to embellish her part. "Chuck is already seated out there, Jen. He thinks I have a major role. What's he going to *say?*"

"It's too late to worry about that now, Liza. The curtain's going up."

By the time the dead came out on stage in Act Three, Liza had finally managed to think of something. Instead of sitting quietly in silence, she coughed, fanned herself with a handkerchief, and occasionally slumped down in her chair as if she were passing out or dying (but since she was already dead, that seemed a little redundant). She still had no lines, but she certainly was *distracting* everyone.

She also made it a point to push herself in front of the entire cast during curtain calls. Christina Riley, who starred as Emily, got real p.o.'d about that.

When it was over, we stopped at Charlie's for sodas. Chuck and Albert didn't say a word. Ingvild was very polite. "Next time, you'll get a much bigger part, I'm sure," she said.

A compliment from Ingvild wasn't what Liza wanted. She craved applause from Chuck, who finally made a comment.

"There's a saying in the theater: 'There are no small parts, only small actors.' But that's a crock. There are definitely small parts, Liza, and yours was the smallest one I've ever seen!"

Chapter Thirteen

"Every day in every way . . ." Well, you know the rest.

There must be a point of no return in things, where you just keep going along the same path, even though you *know* it's leading nowhere—or toward disaster—but you still keep going because you don't know what else to do.

Liza calls that *principle.*

"We can't give up now, Jen," she kept telling me. "It's the principle of the thing."

In a weird way, she was right. Somehow, our whole dumb scheme had nothing to do with Ingvild any longer. We had to prove something to ourselves, even if we dropped dead trying.

Unfortunately, Liza's theatrical debut had put her back a few points with Chuck. According to him, it was okay to have a microscopic part in a *professional* production, but in a high school amateur production, it was *pathetic.* Liza still felt Ingvild might lure Chuck away from her any minute. I told her that was paranoid, since Ingvild didn't go to Chuck's audition and never saw his glossies—never even saw *him*—unless we were all together.

"I don't care," she insisted, "there's a gleam in

Chuck's eye that was never there before. I can sense the vibrations between them."

I knew what she meant. I sensed the same thing between Albert and Ingvild. *He* said he was only being extra nice to her because I'd told him to, but I knew better.

So I recommitted myself to "the cause." When I'd finished my books on vegetarians, I read up on animal rights, animal husbandry, and everything else pertaining to four-legged creatures (A college zoology book proved particularly helpful).

As the weather grew colder, we stopped standing outside Bloomie's on Saturdays. Instead, sometimes me and Albert would stroll through Riverside Park together. That was a perfect opportunity to exhibit my newfound knowledge, especially when Albert fed the squirrels.

"Oh yes," I sighed, "I've always loved the furry creatures in the family Sciuridae."

Albert acquired a blank stare, something I'd been seeing quite often in our recent conversations. "The *what?*"

"The family Sciuridae. That's the group in the order Rodentia to which squirrels belong. Didn't you know *that?*"

"No, Jen. Thanks for telling me."

"Do you realize how they root out the peanuts they bury? By smell. Isn't that *fascinating?*"

"Yeah, sure. How about seeing a movie?"

"Wonderful. There's a silent movie playing at the Museum of Modern Art."

"*Silent?* I thought we'd see one with sound."

"But this one's fascinating, Albert. The man who made it spent years in the Arctic with the Eskimos. It's called *Nanook of the North* and it has dozens of Alaskan huskies in it.''

''All the same, I'd rather go up to Broadway.''

''Why?''

''For one thing, it's closer to home. And I think you're coming down with something.''

''What's *that* mean?''

''It means you've been acting *different* lately, Jen. Have you been taking those allergy pills again?''

Had I gained points on that one or not? At least Albert was concerned about my health. No; who was I kidding? I was taking one step forward and two back.

I simply *had* to boost my ego before that Lovey Face competition. Whenever possible, I'd *visualize* myself in a magazine ad, looking outdoorsy and athletic, holding up a bottle of Lovey Face.

The term *fresh-scrubbed* kept coming back to me, so I tried something drastic. One day I went to school without makeup, hoping that would achieve the natural look required. I knew that plan had failed when everyone asked if I had a cold or my period, or was I contagious.

At school, the mysterious vandals of Fordham were still the hot topic of conversation. By now, Mr. Corbett was furious because they hadn't come forward, so he announced his plan to punish anyone concealing information which would help ''bring them to justice.''

During class breaks everyone talked about it in the hallways. Whenever I worked in the office during study period, I'd hear the secretaries talking about it too. I learned Corbett was compiling a blacklist of students who'd made trouble in the past, along with their associates. That seemed unfair to me. It sounded just like McCarthy's awful Commie scare tactics we'd been reading about in social studies class.

Liza didn't agree. She said she'd squeal instantly if she'd had any information. "Whoever it was ruined our chances with those dreamboats at Fordham." According to her, the fact those jocks never *noticed* us was an unimportant detail. "You're wrong, Liza. If I knew who stole that liquor, I wouldn't want to be punished for not talking."

But most of the time my mind was on more personal things. As I lay in bed at night, peculiarly profound thoughts would surface. Why was I making jealousy my lifetime occupation? Once I dragged out several psychology books Carolyn had left behind, hoping to find an answer. I couldn't decide if I were a manic depressive, a manic compulsive, or just plain manic. I had symptoms of them all.

But one thing was certain. I must've been a good actress. So far, Ingvild didn't suspect any of my dark thoughts. We'd still gab on the bus and chat before going to bed. Oh, we were always sociable and pleasant, but I knew there was something wrong.

By now, that shriveling-up feeling inside me had turned into a permanent knot. I could almost visualize it: a black, lumpy thing somewhere in my midsection.

I asked Liza if she had one too.

"No, why should I? It's a dog-eat-dog world, Jen. We've got to look out for ourselves. Read some self-improvement books and you'll find that out."

No thanks. I was still busy with zoology. Anyway, survival of the fittest *did* seem the way of the world—especially with animals—so I trudged on. But my morale was getting lower.

Morale at school was also at an all-time low. We were sick of having lunch in our homerooms, and the teachers couldn't stand it either. After all, they had to eat with *us.* They found sodas spilled on the floor, wadded-up wrappers in everyone's desks, and uneaten sandwiches in the corners. Then came the disgusting arrival of roaches in the closets.

Corbett was on the loudspeaker daily, complaining about the sudden "infestation." When the school began crawling with bugs, he grew more determined that things get back to normal. He also became obsessed by the idea of "unearthing the culprits who have made the Fordham cafeteria off limits." He began putting on more pressure. "Anyone who knows *anything* must come forward, or be considered equally guilty."

So far, no one had blabbed, but we all discussed the problem. Once on our way home from school, I brought up the subject. "It's—well, *unethical.* I mean, if someone happens to know who did it, why should they be equally to blame?"

Albert didn't agree. "If someone knows who did it, it's a moral obligation to speak out. Doing nothing makes him or her an accessory, just like Corbett says."

Liza thought so too. "Doing nothing makes us *all* suffer. Meanwhile, our classrooms are gross. A roach walked right across my math book this morning."

Beryl shuddered. "I can't stand roaches. I can't even eat raisin bread, or dates."

"Don't be so graphic," Liza groaned.

"What's wrong with roaches?" asked Albert. He still had fond memories of them as pets when he was in first grade. "They're prehistoric, and they'll survive us all because they can adapt."

"But I don't choose to adapt to *them,*" Beryl argued.

Ingvild didn't say anything.

I felt the conversation had gotten twisted around. "I merely wanted to make a point. Guilt by association is *wrong.*"

"Let's change the subject," said Beryl, "to a far more scintillating one. That Lovey Face audition is coming up two weeks from Saturday. The company is sending an announcement to all the high schools. Since Corbett has been such a demon lately, I bet he won't post it, so I'm delivering the word in person." She glanced at me and Ingvild. "You guys are definitely trying out, aren't you?"

I glanced at Liza. "Maybe," I said.

"Of course you're trying out," insisted Liza.

Ingvild didn't say anything. She'd been unusually quiet for *days.*

"What's wrong?" I asked.

"Nothing. I think I'll go to the library now. See you later." Then she walked away.

"Hasn't Ingvild been acting odd lately?" asked Beryl.

Albert shrugged. "Who knows? I've given up trying to figure you girls out."

"It must be the roaches," she concluded. "I'll bet they don't have any in Norway."

It wasn't the roaches. Something was on Ingvild's mind, and I knew what it was.

"She *suspects* the way I feel," I told Liza. "The past few days, Ingvild hasn't spent any time with me. She's always off at the library. I know she's avoiding me, Liza, and I don't blame her. The whole thing came to me in a flash last night. I was baby-sitting for Eric Malone, reading him *Snow White.* Suddenly, *I* was the evil queen, trying to kill off my prettier rival. It made me feel creepy."

"Don't overdramatize," said Liza. "Which reminds me, I got a part in the next school play—a *real* part this time. Sixteen lines. That should impress Chuck; it's fifteen more lines than he's ever had."

"Haven't you been *listening?*"

"Sure. Take my advice, Jen, be your own best friend and keep polishing your ego, too. Lovey Face is just around the corner. But I've a super idea that'll make us *both* feel terrific."

"Which is?"

"Haven't you noticed? It's snowing. The first snowfall of the season."

I glanced out the window. "So?"

"It's also Friday. The weather report says this'll keep up all weekend."

"Who cares?"

"*We* do. Have you forgotten those gorgeous jocks, Patrick and Ron? They always go skiing on the golf course in Van Cortland park when it snows."

"You mean we should . . ."

"What else? Getting a date with them would make Albert and Chuck take notice and improve our self-images considerably. But first we'll have to rent cross-country skis —unless you happen to have two pair hanging around."

Chapter Fourteen

Look, I *agreed* with Liza. Honestly. It *was* a good idea. Impressing Patrick and Ron would make us feel terrific: the perfect way to boost my ego prior to the Lovey Face audition. I'd planned to get a facial and listen to a self-improvement tape, but this was much better. After all, athletes psych themselves up before competition, right? Aspiring models should, too.

I immediately mentioned Carolyn's skis, just going to waste in our basement; naturally, Liza knew about them, anyway. As for the minor detail that we didn't know how to ski, Liza thought it insignificant.

"How hard can it be? It's probably just like walking with boards on your feet."

Maybe so, but I figured we should read up on skiing first. On Saturday morning, we went back to the library for more books. If nothing else, I was becoming well informed.

"See, I told you," said Liza, "it says here the chances of breaking a leg on skis is a thousand to one. Anyone can learn. Even toddlers can ski, and cross-country skiing is the easiest."

"How can we be sure Patrick and Ron will be there?"

"They're *always* there, I overheard them say so . . . every Sunday at twelve. So we'll be there too."

That afternoon we rummaged through the basement storage room and found the skis and poles, neatly tucked away. But no ski boots.

"Now what?" I asked. "Carolyn must've packed her boots in the trunk, and I don't have the key. Maybe we can wear our jogging shoes."

"Hardly. We'll *rent* boots."

"Where?"

"In the park, of course. They have rentals there; I called to check.

"Then let's rent skis there, too. If Carolyn discovers I borrowed hers, she'll kill me. These are her prized possessions."

"Precisely why we need them, silly. Rental skis are probably tacky. Ski buffs are nutso about their equipment, Jen. Terrific skis like this will impress Patrick and Ron, and that's the name of the game, right?"

As I stood in the basement surrounded by tenants' air conditioners, bicycles, and trunks, I visualized myself scooting along newly packed snow, feeling fresh scrubbed, athletic, and confident, waving to Patrick and Ron in the distance. I was the ideal image Lovey Face was searching for!

"Okay," I agreed.

"Where are you going in this dreadful weather?" asked Mom.

I was wearing my down jacket, plus two layers of tights under my jeans. "To the Bronx," I told her.

"To the zoo? Maybe Ingvild would like to come along."

Luckily, Ingvild said she couldn't. She had other things to do.

"Tell Albert to get you home by five," said Mom. "We're having an early dinner."

I met Liza downstairs, as arranged. We picked up the skis in the basement, then carried them to the Broadway subway. Snow had fallen all night, so the streets were a slushy mess. Struggling down the subway steps, we held the skis over our heads, then pushed through the turnstile. We rammed into several people as we maneuvered through the subway doors. By the time we'd reached 242nd Street, we'd received lots of filthy looks.

"All ski buffs must have *cars,*" I concluded.

As we headed toward the golf course, the snow kept falling heavily. I was anxious to get there, imagining a deserted pastoral landscape covered in white.

Hardly! Everyone in New York was there in full force. I'd never seen so many woolen hats with pom-poms. Tons of cars crowded the parking lot, and dozens of little kids spilled out, carrying ski equipment.

Liza was confident. "See? If they can maneuver these dumb skis, *we* certainly can."

First we stopped at the rental shop to pick up ski boots. "I didn't realize they'd be so *big,*" I said, staring at the clumsy, clunky things.

"Be sure you get the proper size," said the man behind the counter.

He had no time to help us, so we chose by ourselves after trying several pair.

"I feel like Frankenstein," I grumbled. "How can we look glamorous in these? They weigh a ton."

Liza chose a pair that looked too tight, and mine felt much too big. After we'd paid the rental and admission fee, we headed toward a hill, already filled with people, to watch how they clamped their boots to their skis, then attached the bindings.

"That looks simple enough," said Liza.

I didn't think so. "Let's ask an instructor."

"No, we'll look like *amateurs.*"

I attached my boots to the skis, which made my feet feel they were buried in two buckets of cement with giant oars sticking out each end.

"See, that wasn't hard," said Liza, digging her poles into the snow.

I dug mine in, too, but they quickly sunk into the ground. Fortunately, the ten-ton boots kept me from falling on my face. As I regained my balance, a punky little kid rear-ended me with his skis. Then he stuck a pole in my rib and shouted, "Turkey."

"Don't mind him," said Liza. " 'Turkey' is a ski expression, meaning amateur. Try not to look so *frightened.*" She took a deep breath of cold air. "Isn't this invigorating, Jen?"

We glanced around at the mass of people hoping to spy Patrick and Ron. But looking for two jocks in a crowd of skiers is like searching for a needle in a haystack. With the snow falling, I was almost blinded.

As we trudged on, I felt the circulation in my legs start cutting off. I also had a weird pain in both my shins. When that began to go away, I started getting numb.

Liza scooted up ahead of me, digging her poles into the snow.

"I'm freezing," I said, trying to catch up.

"You have no gloves, stupid. No one goes skiing without gloves."

She could've told me that before we left the house, right? After a while, my hands resembled raw meat; then they got numb too. Soon, every part of me was either numb, aching, or frostbitten.

Why was no one else having problems? Old ladies skied past me and little kids tripped me up. When I glanced back to measure the distance I'd traveled, it looked like five feet.

"Don't stop now," shouted Liza, "you'll cause a bottleneck."

For sure. There were so many people slooshing around on the snow, it looked like a ski marathon. Like Mom says, there's nothing you can do in the city *alone.*

"This is hopeless," I panted. "I think I'm getting snow fever *and* snow blindness. We'll never meet two jocks in this crowd, anyway."

"O ye of little faith. Glance over there and tell me what you see, Jennifer."

I was hoping it'd be a Saint Bernard with a rescue flask of cocoa. Instead I saw two guys up ahead, one wearing a bright yellow ski outfit, the other all in white. "It's either a snow mirage or Patrick and Ron."

"And you thought we'd *never* find them. We'll just ski along beside them and ask for a few professional pointers. Before you know it, we'll all be doing the après-ski bit together in some coffee house. I promise."

I was having trouble hearing; my ears had frozen

123

solid. My head was pounding and every muscle in my legs throbbed. Still, I made the valiant effort to maneuver myself in their direction, while snow kept pelting me in the face.

Liza moved into action. She pulled up short, just inches from Patrick and Ron, then accidentally on purpose dropped her poles by their boots. That caused me to run into her from behind and drop mine too. For a moment, we both teetered back and forth like topsy-turvey dolls, unable to regain our balance. We wound up falling into one another, after which we bumped into the two jocks.

"Watch it, will you," said Ron, brushing himself off.

"Excuse me." Liza smiled. "My friend is a beginner."

"That's no secret," said Patrick. "She has her rattraps on all wrong. And so do you."

"Really? What could I have been *thinking* of?"

I stared down at my feet, wondering which part of the overall mess was a rattrap.

"Tell me," Liza continued, "don't we know each other from somewhere?"

Patrick and Ron stared blankly. It was obvious our many lunch hours spent drooling at these guys had made absolutely no impression.

Ron handed Liza back her poles. "You're both going to blow out of those bindings any minute."

Patrick agreed. "You've got the wrong size boots, too." He pointed to Liza. "You have hot spots." Then he turned to me and added, "And you have slop."

"Those bails look touch and go too," Ron added.

I couldn't understand a word they were saying, but their attitude was certainly condescending. Apparently, nothing angers a ski buff more than a poorly turned out, ill-equipped beginner.

Patrick looked disgusted. "Who outfitted you kids, anyway, the grim reaper? Get the hell off the course before you kill yourselves!"

Then Ron mumbled something about "inexperienced, amateur *idiots*," and they both turned their skis around and headed down the hill.

Liza was furious. She lifted her ski in the air to kick snow in their direction. Instead, her ski came down with a thud, landing on *my* ski.

I nearly cried when I heard the *crunch;* I would've, but the tears might've frozen on my face. "You *broke* it, stupid," I shouted, staring down at what was left of my sister's prized possession.

Liza looked equally upset. "Sorry, Jen. Maybe you can glue it together or something. Please don't be mad at me —I feel bad enough already. Who would've guessed those jocks would turn out to be such utter *jerks*!"

The day went "downhill" after that, pardon the pun. When we returned our boots to the rental shop, we discovered our feet were red, raw, and covered with blisters. (caused by "slop" and "hot spots," I guess). The snow suddenly turned to sleet, so we were soaked to the skin by the time we reached the subway station. The bad weather had delayed the trains and we had to stand around and wait for half an hour, during which time I imagined Carolyn thousands of miles away getting psychic visions of her mutilated skis.

We arrived home way after five, so Mom's dinner was ruined. Albert had called twice, which meant Mom knew I hadn't been to the zoo after all. I told her I'd changed my mind and gone to see a horror movie with Liza—about abominable snowmen.

Which, come to think of it, was only half a lie.

Chapter Fifteen

Enough already, right? I mean, only an *idiot* would continue on a collision course with disaster, even for a principle.

By now, I felt like visualizing Liza right out of my life! All her grand schemes had left me feeling *more* inferior.

I didn't want to compete any longer, *truly.* But that hard little knot inside—which had become my alter ego—kept insisting I do *something* to improve my self-esteem before the Lovey Face audition on Saturday. Something; but *what*? Plastic surgery, perhaps?

No, my outsides were fine. The way I felt *inside* was destroying my self-esteem. It'd require *major* surgery to remove that knot of jealousy.

You know that awful feeling you have when you're hiding something from someone but you think they probably know anyway? I had that too. I was convinced Ingvild sensed my envy and had been avoiding me. I mean, we barely spoke at *all* anymore.

The only thing that took my mind off the whole mess was the even bigger mess at school. A group of students started protesting outside Corbett's office, insisting he immediately do something about the unsanitary lunch conditions created by eating in our classrooms or else they'd call the Board of Education *and* the Board of Health. In addition, the student council had formed a grievance committee to picket outside school. They demanded amnesty for anyone knowing the identity of the thieves in the Fordham cafeteria caper. Apparently, lots of kids shared my opinion about that.

Within a few days, Emerson started looking like one of those college campuses during the sixties protests. I half expected some students to take over the building and begin a hunger strike or something.

Then on Wednesday, Corbett made another announcement over the loudspeaker:

"The remainder of the new plumbing is being installed this weekend. Auditorium and cafeteria facilities will be functioning normally again on Monday. In addition, we now have evidence regarding the vandalism at Fordham. The students involved will report to school this Saturday morning, with parents or guardians. I consider all ongoing protests ill-advised and hope all Emerson students will now return to their academic obligations."

Corbett may've discovered the vandals, but he wasn't telling who they were. Lots of students didn't believe him anyway. They thought it was a tactic to put an end to their protests. Members of the student council refused to stop picketing.

That afternoon I was scheduled to do some filing in the office during study period. As I was leaving math class, Victor Mackenzie, president of the student council, stopped me in the hall. Victor is a real intense type, who can't wait to get into Harvard to study law so he can start revolutionizing the legal system.

"Wait up, Beaumont. I heard you're working in Corbett's office today, is that right?"

"Yeah."

He glanced over his shoulder to assure himself no one was listening. "Well you'd be doing the council a big favor if you'd keep your eyes and ears open, okay?"

"What for?"

"Did you come from Mars or what? For *information.* The council wants to make sure Corbett actually knows who the vandals are. If he does, *we'll* be around to make sure their civil rights aren't violated."

"Listen," I argued, "I just do filing."

"Even so, you might hear something. If you do, we'd like to know exactly what it is. Enough said?"

"Sure . . . I guess so."

Victor nodded knowingly, winked, then hurried down the hall. Our brief conversation had made me feel like a double agent or something.

When I arrived at the office, Mrs. Rosenfeld had a stack of folders waiting to be put away. The filing cabinet is against the wall between the outer office and Corbett's office. His door is usually open, which meant if anything was said, I was sure to hear it. So I listened.

First I heard him talking with the gym teacher. They were making arrangements for the annual dance in the auditorium. That thing is always a bust because only dopes and losers show up to stand around and drink watery Hawaiian Punch.

When Farley left, Mrs. Rosenfeld went in, and the conversation got more interesting. They began talking about the vandals responsible for the Fordham theft. Mrs. Rosenfeld closed the door halfway, so I inched closer to the wall.

"Are you certain all three have confessed?" asked Corbett. "I don't want our student council suggesting I used coercion. Those kids love to take an adversary position."

"Yes," said Mrs. Rosenfeld. "Lara Ogilvy spoke with the guidance counselor yesterday. She convinced Kim Rainey and Donna Fitzgerald to come forward as well."

So the Terrible Three were the vandals! I should've known it'd been those weirdos who'd screwed up the entire school!

Mrs. Rosenfeld closed the door all the way; the conversation was muffled but I could still make out what she said. "As for Ingvild Larsen," she continued, "she wasn't actually a participant, but the girls confided in her. She's known who the vandals were for quite some time."

What? Had I heard *Ingvild's* name? I inched closer to the door, gluing my ear against the wall.

"Larsen?" asked Corbett. "Isn't she that foreign exchange student?"

"That's right. Her academic record is good, but she hasn't been here long enough for us to know much about her character. Don't you think it's unwise to hold her accountable too? After all, the other girls admitted she wasn't even there. They told her about the robbery because she's a friend."

I heard a moment's silence before Corbett answered.

"I see your point, Miriam. But I can't retract my original decision, even though the student council will probably pound down my door. Especially Mackenzie—that kid thinks he's Clarence Darrow. No; I've already said any student withholding information will be punished. Who is Ingvild Larsen living with?''

"She's staying with Mrs. Beaumont and her daughter. Jennifer is a sophomore here. In fact, she's working in the outer office now.''

"Well, don't mention this to her. But you'll have to call Mrs. Beaumont and explain the entire mess. I want all four girls in my office Saturday morning.''

As Mrs. Rosenfeld left Corbett's office, I hurried to the other side of the room. I began shoving envelopes around her desk, trying to look busy until the bell sounded.

"Thank you, Jennifer," she said. "You can go to your next class now.''

I left the office in a daze, still not believing what I'd heard. Ingvild had known who the thieves were all along! No wonder she kept silent whenever we discussed the robbery. She was an accessory—and Corbett planned to hold her equally accountable. What did that mean? I wondered. Would Ingvild be expelled, put on detention, be marked down, or what?

As I walked down the hall, still stunned by the news, the impact of the rest of what Corbett had said suddenly hit me. Saturday morning. Ingvild was to be in his office on *Saturday morning.*

That was the morning of the Lovey Face audition.

No one can be in two places at once, right? All my weeks of worry about competing with Ingvild for that job had been unnecessary. She wouldn't be able to try out for it after all. Fate had stepped in and put the odds in *my* favor, for a change.

Ingvild was out of the running.

Come Saturday morning, I'd be in the offices of Lovey Face, looking well groomed, fresh-scrubbed, and confident, and Ingvild would be cooling her heels in Corbett's office, waiting for the axe to fall.

But that was justice, I suppose.

As I headed for the biology lab, Victor Mackenzie ran down the hall and grabbed my arm.

"Did you find out anything, Beaumont?"

I stared at him as if he weren't there. "What?"

"Does Corbett have the goods on anyone or not? Our organization is all geared up to step in. The student council here needs more clout, and this is our rallying point. I could work up a defense overnight if only I knew some *facts*. Corbett thinks he can bypass jurisprudence, but everyone deserves their day in court. We don't want any storm-trooper tactics being used this weekend."

"What do you mean?"

Victor was getting impatient. "Names, Beaumont, we need *names*. The council has agreed no one should be threatened with expulsion. We'd like to prevent that, but we need to know who the accused parties are. Well? Did you learn anything?"

Victor's high-powered speech had thrown me off guard, but one thing was clear. If I told him the names of the "accused," he'd do everything in his power to prevent that confrontation scheduled for Saturday.

I *couldn't* tell him. If I did, Ingvild would be free that Saturday, free to compete with me for Lovey Face, free to *win*—so I lied.

"Sorry, Victor. I didn't learn anything."

He shrugged. "Well, we're not giving up," he said, and walked away.

I began feeling queazy and faint and started to perspire, so instead of going to biology class, I hurried to the bathroom to wash my face. I splashed cold water all over it, then stared at myself in the mirror.

A stranger stared back.

I blinked and stared again, but I still wasn't seeing Jenny Beaumont. It may've been the wicked stepsister in Cinderella or the evil queen in Snow White, but it wasn't me. It was a deceitful, envious little creature who'd stop at nothing to get her way.

That's when I knew I was staring at the face of jealousy, in all its hoptoad, fire-eating ugliness.

And I hated what I saw.

Chapter Sixteen

I knew I had to talk with Ingvild.

I was still in a daze when I returned to the biology lab. I glanced around, but Ingvild wasn't there. She wasn't in French class, either. Mrs. Hirsch said Ingvild hadn't felt well, so she'd gotten an early dismissal pass. After French, I cut gym and took the bus home.

The house was quiet when I arrived. I called out Ingvild's name, but she didn't answer. I found her in our bedroom, lying in the dark. When I switched on the light I could see she'd been crying.

"Go away, Jennifer," she sobbed, "leave me alone."

I paid no attention. "Why didn't you *tell* me about this mess? Why'd you cover up for those creeps who stole the liquor?"

She rubbed her eyes. "How did you find out?"

"I overheard everything in Corbett's office this afternoon. It's true, isn't it?"

She turned her face away, too embarrassed to look at me. "Yes, it's true. I knew they were the thieves. Lara told me, but I didn't *want* to know about it. I thought it was all right to keep quiet, but now it has become a bad thing. Oh, no one understands. I can't even write my parents.

They mustn't know I'm in trouble. What's going to happen to me?''

She began crying again. I'd never seen Ingvild so upset, so I tried to calm her down. "Listen, it's not as bad as you think."

"You don't understand. Coming to New York meant so much to me. I wanted to be a new person, with new people. Always at home, I feel . . . Oh, I can't explain it, it all sounds so silly."

I thought maybe I knew what she meant. "You wanted a new image? That's not silly. I felt the same way when my sister left. I was hoping my life would be totally different."

"No, that's only part of it," she insisted.

"Okay, I'm listening. What's the rest?"

She sat up on the bed and blew her nose. "It's no use. I don't have the *words*."

"Sure you do."

"Well . . . since I've come here, I have been—pretending. Always I'm pretending, but now it has become too hard and I've made a mess of things. I wanted so much to be popular."

I didn't know what she meant. "But you are. You're one of the most popular girls at school. Everyone likes you."

"They don't." she shouted. "Not really."

"Of course they do."

"No," she insisted, "no one likes me—not the *real* me. Not even the girls on the volleyball team."

Ingvild wasn't making sense. "What are you talking about? You won the big game for them. You were the *star*."

135

"I know," she sobbed, her voice shaking, "but now they resent me and I don't know *why.* I always try to be so nice to them all, and to their friends too."

As the major victim of Ingvild's "niceness" I knew it could drive a person crazy. "Well, maybe you've been *too* nice. A perfect person makes everyone else feel rotten, you know? Anyway, why didn't you tell me all this stuff before? After all, we're supposed to be your family while you're here."

"Oh Jenny, you still don't understand *anything,*" she argued. "Always, I write my parents to tell them how well I'm doing. All these weeks I've worked so hard, and now everything is ruined. I wanted my parents to be *proud* of me. Always, they are more proud of my brothers than of me. They say my brothers are smarter, more popular. My brothers will go to a fine university, but not me. So I work extra hard to impress them, to make them notice *me* too—make them think I'm special. To be a foreign exchange student, that would be very special, I thought, and something my brothers have never done. But now I've done a wrong thing, and when they find out about it, they will send me home."

Send her home? A little earlier I might've thought that was a great idea: the answer to all my problems. But now I knew better. Making Ingvild look bad wouldn't solve my problem. *I* was my problem. During the bus ride home, I'd figured that out. I'd thought over all the wacky things me and Liza had done over the past few weeks and I knew none of it had made me a better person—only a bigger jerk.

"No one's sending you home," I insisted. "I told you

we'd work things out. Look, I know just how you feel, because I feel the same way."

Ingvild shook her head. "No, Jenny, we are not the same. For you, things are *easy*."

"Are you kidding? You're much smarter than me."

"But it's a *lie*. I feel I must get good marks, so I work extra hard. Sometimes at night when you're asleep, I wake up and study. Yes, I do many things, but only because I need to make people like me. With you, it's different. People like you just the way you are. You don't have to always *prove* yourself. If you get a bad grade, your mother isn't angry at you. Those girls you call weirdos understand these things. At home, they have many problems, too, so I can talk to them. I can stop pretending."

"Why should you pretend? You have lots of friends. Kids from your study group are always calling."

She burst into tears again. "That's because I haven't gone," she confessed. "Oh, I've told so many lies. That group was much too hard for me, so I dropped out. All this time when I said I was in the library, I was really with those three girls. They are my only real friends."

"Look, Ingvild, maybe I haven't been such a terrific friend, but it's not because I didn't want to be. When you first came everything was great. But when you started being so fantastic at everything—well, I felt jealous. But I couldn't talk with you about it because I also felt real guilty. I was mad because you were getting all the attention."

"See, I've made *you* hate me, too," she moaned. "I told you I've done everything wrong. Always, my mother tells me I'm not sociable enough. So when I came here, I decided to be different, more friendly. I helped your mother with the house so you'd both be glad I was here. But all these things take work, and there is also so much schoolwork. I only pretend it's easy for me."

"C'mon. You got a terrific grade on that English paper."

"Because I'd read that play before. Also, I understand the character of Nora—*her* life was a lie too. You say you've been jealous of me, but I'm the one who's jealous. I envy you, Jenny. You don't need to lie to be liked. I even lied to Chuck."

"What about?"

"I never acted in a school play. Liza said to pretend I was interested in acting, so I did. But I don't really know anything about the theater. In our little town, there's no such thing as theater."

"But that's silly. Why would you—"

"Don't you see? I wanted Liza to like me better too. Sometimes when you're both together, I think you're laughing at me. When I first came, I said I wanted us to be true friends, friends who talk to each other. I thought you wanted that, too, but suddenly you pulled away from me. So I tried being nicer, but you kept pulling away. That's when I made friends with Lara and Kim and Donna. I felt they would accept me because they had no other friends."

"Yeah well, that's because they're *creeps*."

"But they're not, Jenny. They have problems, too. Donna's parents just got divorced, and she was feeling unhappy, so she did a bad thing. When they stole the liquor, Lara told me about it but made me promise not to say anything. Then Mr. Corbett said *that* was bad too. But I *couldn't* tell anyone. Oh, I've made a mess of everything!"

After Ingvild had finished blurting things out, she threw herself onto the bed again in silence.

I felt like kicking myself. I'd been a stupid fool for listening to Liza's crazy ideas— No. I couldn't blame Liza; I'd been just as stupid.

"You're right," I agreed, "things *are* a mess. But it's not all your fault. If only you hadn't been so nice to Albert! I thought you were trying to take him away from me. Liza thought the same thing about Chuck. After all, being friendly and flirting are two different things."

"Flirting?" she shouted, looking a little hysterical. "That's not what I meant to do! I listened to Chuck's long stories because Liza asked me to, even though I think he's terribly conceited. And I read all Albert's pamphlets, even though they have terrible pictures of dead animals inside. What's wrong with me? Can't I do *anything* right?"

"Okay, I was wrong; you weren't flirting. But when you got interested in *my* Lovey Face competition, I really went nuts."

"*I* never mentioned Lovey Face—*Beryl* did!"

"True, but you were planning to try out for it, weren't you? I mean, you *want* to, right?"

Ingvild wiped a few remaining tears from her face, then stared at me. "You don't know what I want, or what I like, do you, Jenny? Because you never really *asked* me."

I supposed that was true. "Okay, so I'm asking you now. Do you want to try out for the modeling contract or not?"

"I want to be an athlete."

"A what?"

"Yes, an athlete. Well, I'd like to teach athletics someday. My brothers, they are much finer athletes, but I don't care if I'm not the best; it's what I've always wanted. When I go to college, I wish to learn to become a physical education teacher."

"So how come you never told me that?"

"Always, I'm afraid to be laughed at. You said you hated sports, so I thought you'd think to be a gym teacher is a silly thing. You always laugh at the gym teacher at school and call him stupid."

"But that's so dumb, Ingvild."

"I know," she agreed. "I'm dumb and I've made a terrible mess of things."

"No, I mean things have gotten real twisted around because we haven't *talked* to each other. Listen, even if you don't want to be a model for life, you should try out for the contract anyway. If you win you'll earn lots of money to use for college."

"You just said you didn't want me to try out!"

"Sure, I don't *want* to compete with you, but you should go for it anyway. When I first learned you were involved in the vandalism, I was glad—because it meant you'd be in Corbett's office Saturday, so you couldn't beat me out at the audition."

"You want to win that badly?"

"I suppose I do."

Ingvild was getting more confused. "Then why are you telling me to go?"

"Because winning like that isn't really winning—I finally realize that. Don't you see?"

"No, I don't. But it doesn't matter, I *can't* go. On Saturday, I must be in school to take my punishment."

"No you won't," I told her. "The student council won't allow that. The whole thing's unfair, anyway. After all, you didn't do anything. I'm calling Victor Mackenzie right now. He'll have the whole deal cleared up in no time, wait and see."

Victor sounded even more militant than I'd hoped. "Good work, Beaumont. I'll get our forces into action right away. Sit tight and I'll call you back."

"See," I told Ingvild, "it's not half as terrible as it seems."

She was still real worried. "If only I didn't have to write my parents about this."

"Look, maybe there'll be nothing to write them about. C'mon. Let's start dinner while we wait for Victor to call back."

As we rummaged around the kitchen, Ingvild's mood gradually picked up. I found enough leftovers to put together a decent dinner, while she set the table. Suddenly I was starving. "I'm so hungry I can eat my own food," I joked. That familiar ugly knot inside me had finally gone away. Discovering Ingvild wasn't the perfect person I'd imagined had made all the difference. "Have you really been getting up late at night to study?" I asked.

"All the time," she admitted. "Many subjects are difficult, and in English they are *worse*. French is the only thing that isn't hard. But I promised my parents I'd do well in everything, so always in my letters, I tell them that."

As I tossed the salad, I thought of Carolyn's lengthy letters and wondered if things were actually as great as she always made out. Maybe things were hard for everyone— even Carolyn.

"Always, I feel pressured," Ingvild continued, "because my brothers do everything so well. It's hard to get attention."

"Same here. Isn't it ironic? We're exactly the same, actually, only we didn't know it. Anyway, I feel good now that things are out in the open."

"I wanted to tell you before, Jenny, but I couldn't. You seemed to think everything was so easy for me, so I just let you."

"I wanted to have things out with you, too. So did Liza. But you were so absolutely perfect all the time, we made fools of ourselves instead. We even tried getting dates with those jocks from Fordham, but we messed up totally."

Ingvild managed a laugh. "I'm glad I'm not the only one who made a mess of things."

"Don't worry, you've got company. You should've seen what idiots me and Liza were!"

As I finished heating up dinner, Ingvild started pacing around the kitchen. "Will your friend call back soon you think?"

"Don't worry, Victor will straighten things out."

A little later when the phone rang, I rushed to answer it. It was Victor, saying he had things under control. That guy is a real powerhouse. He'd called Kim Rainey's father, a lawyer, and together they'd thrashed the whole thing out. Then he'd called the principal at home.

"Corbett just accepted our terms," he explained. "The three girls won't be expelled, just put on suspension, as long as they agree to see the guidance counselor every week and make a formal apology to the staff at Fordham."

"And Ingvild?"

"She's off the hook. I threw in some junk about contacting the Norwegian Consulate, but it wasn't necessary. I think Corbett was looking for a way to back off gracefully, but he needed to be pressured into it. He's been getting a bad rep at the district office since we've been picketing. Anyway, no heads will roll this Saturday. Tell your friend we've arranged a permanent reprieve."

"Thanks a million, Victor, you did a great job."

"Yeah, for an ad hoc committee we didn't do badly, considering it was actually a prima facie case. But once I'd convinced Corbett the theft lacked animus furandi, I had him."

"Lacked what?"

"Animus furandi: the *intention* of stealing. In other words, it wasn't premeditated. The girls just wanted attention, so they did a stupid thing, you know?"

"Yeah, Victor. I definitely know all about *that*."

During dinner, Ingvild and I told Mom everything. I even mentioned Carolyn's broken skis, which was really big of me, I thought, considering she probably wouldn't discover the fact until the following winter. But once the truth starts pouring out you can't put a stopper on it.

"Me and Ingvild have wasted lots of time," I said, "but now we're going to start all over."

Mom was overwhelmed. "I'd no idea all this was going on, but I'm proud of you both for coming to terms with it. I also had no idea you felt inferior to Carolyn. Maybe you and I haven't been communicating enough, either. I'm sorry, Jenny." Then Mom threw in lots of comments about my maturing through a difficult learning experience and discovering the true meaning of friendship and other overly syrupy, social-worky stuff like that, but I didn't mind. They were compliments, and I loved hearing them.

"I'm just glad it's over," sighed Ingvild. "I would've *died* if I had to go to school on Saturday."

"Right," I said, digging into the salad, which I'd managed to make quite edible. "Especially since we both have more important business this Saturday."

"Oh?" asked Mom, "what's that?"

"Ingvild and I are trying out for the Lovey Face contract," I explained. *"Together."*

Chapter Seventeen

By nine o'clock Saturday morning, I'd already changed my clothes four times. First I was formal, then casual, then sporty. By nine thirty I'd settled on a combination of all three and was finally satisfied.

"I look awful," groaned Ingvild, staring at herself in the mirror.

"Don't start again," I argued. "I'm not a dentist. It was like pulling teeth to convince you to come in the first place."

"But my hair," she whined. "Look at it."

I looked at it. It was blond, silky, and beautiful—as always.

"And my clothes," she grumbled. "They're so . . ."

"They're terrific. That sweater looks great with those slacks and those boots look great with that sweater. Aren't you going to compliment me on *my* outfit?" I'd tried remembering all the fashion instructions Beryl had given me —be bold, be daring, be innovative, make a statement— but at the last minute I'd decided to ignore it all and wear what felt good, namely, an oversize silk shirt, baggy jeans, and my pink leather jazz shoes.

"What do you think?" I asked. "Does it work?"

"Oh yes," Ingvild said admiringly.

I was slipping my lucky penny into the pocket of my jeans when Liza called. "What am I supposed to tell you?" she asked. "Good luck, or break a leg?"

"Good luck sounds lots better."

"You got it—both of you. You're lucky Lovey Face doesn't need a dark curly-haired girl with thick thighs, or I'd be heavy competition." Liza was being a real sweetheart. Now that she knew Ingvild thought Chuck was a conceited egotist, she could afford to be gracious. "What are you wearing?" she asked.

"My beige silk shirt."

"The oversize one? Terrific. Don't forget to splash on lots of perfume. It'll make you feel luxurious."

I forgot. I was in such a state when we dashed out of the house, I was lucky to remember where we were going.

We were supposed to be at the Hilton by eleven o'clock. I was so anxious to get there, we arrived at ten thirty. I figured a representative from Lovey Face would probably be checking out the applicants in the lobby or something. When we were told they were holding interviews in the grand ballroom, I began wondering how big a deal this would turn out to be.

A *very big* deal. The entire room was filled with teenagers—all blond, all poised, all gorgeous. I mean, I'd never seen anything like it. Where had they all come from? After all, it was just a crummy little notice posted on the bulletin board of local high schools. (I'd soon discover that "little" press release had gone out to schools across the country!)

Anyway, as the two of us walked through the door, we were greeted by a guard who handed us each a numbered sticker. Our numbers were 264 and 265. "Take a seat and wait until you're called," he said.

"I think this'll be a *long* wait," I whispered.

There were tons of folding chairs set up around the room underneath the gleaming crystal chandeliers. A long runway, draped in felt, extended from the stage. Seated at either side of the runway behind two long rows of tables were over a dozen men and women, all executive types. They seemed very professional and serious, sort of like a jury.

"I shouldn't have come," said Ingvild nervously. "Look Jenny, there are so many girls—all pretty blondes."

"Not all *natural*," I observed, trying to keep both our spirits up. "Check out number two twelve. Bleached."

I eyed the rest of the competition: definitely great-looking. Everyone was dressed differently, some in casual outfits, some in tight slinky dresses and stiletto heels, and they ranged in height from under five feet to almost six feet: a true convention of teenage blondes. "If they all think they stand a chance, so do we," I reasoned.

Honestly, I don't know what'd come over me. There I was sharing a room with some of the best-looking blondes alive and still thinking I had a shot at that Lovey Face contract. Was I going nuts or what?

As the line finally began moving, each girl went up to speak with the executives or judges or whatever they were. Ingvild and I were handed a form to be filled out. Our vital statistics had to be listed, along with our school, our hobbies, our future plans, and all sorts of other junk I didn't think was anybody's business. Ingvild put down her weight in stones or meters or something, which looked peculiar. Number two sixty-six, seated next to us, leaned over. "Hey, you've gotta weigh more than that—my *cat* weighs more than that!" She smiled. "My name's Donna. Waiting is the pits, don't you agree? Where are you girls from?"

At first glance, Donna struck me as a short, blond Betty Boop type who might've fallen off her high heels once too often.

"I'm from Manhattan," I said.

"And I'm from Norway," said Ingvild.

"Say, that's what I call a *commute*. You must want this contract real bad, right?" Donna took out her compact to apply another layer of lipstick. "I thought driving in from Jersey was bad, but *Norway*. No wonder I haven't seen you before. I make all the rounds all the time."

"You do?" I asked.

"Sure, you have to. Twice a week my Mom drives me into the city. She makes appointments for me with magazine editors, fashion buyers—anyone who uses teenage models. It's not always easy to know what they're looking for, so I keep changing my image. Even so, it's rough breaking into this business. My mom's already spent a fortune, but it'll probably take a few more years."

"Years?"

"Sure, that's what my mom says. I've been at this since I was seven. That's when I started going to the A Plus Charm School."

"How old are you now?" asked Ingvild.

"Fourteen. But sometimes I lie and make myself older —or younger. It depends. You've gotta know what they're looking for first, ya know?"

I was about to ask how anyone could study charm for *seven years* when some girl two rows ahead of us began having a fit or something. She insisted someone had deliberately stepped on her white leather boots and a guard rushed over to calm her down. "I'm sorry," she apologized, "but I'm feeling very emotional right now."

For sure. I was beginning to feel heavy vibes in the place, what with everyone sitting around psyching themselves up for the big moment, hoping they'd pass inspection.

Then suddenly the whole mood in the grand ballroom changed, as a mess of press photographers walked in and began popping flashbulbs. All the executives perked up. Floodlights were turned on and a giant screen was wheeled onstage, onto which shots of Lovey Face products were projected. A woman draped in black chiffon, wearing a feathered hat, walked to the podium and began speaking. "We welcome you all to the Lovey Face Model Competition, in which we hope to find the quintessential image for our prestigious line of cosmetics. Let me take this opportunity to wish you all the best of luck. As you meet representatives of our company, they will be judging you on projection, style, personality, and appropriateness. I must ask you not to engage in conversation with any of our judges, except to answer their questions. Each judge will be giving you a score of from one through twenty-five. These numbers will be noted in ink so figures can't be tampered with. We invite the members of the press to await our final decision, which will come after all the contestants have made their trip down the runway. So remember girls, as you walk by the judges, try to encapsule every mood, emotion, and attitude you feel about yourself. We know that somewhere out there is our Lovey Face!"

A contestant near me groaned. "I just can't feel good about myself under these conditions!"

I knew what she meant. Only, by some miracle, my usual nervous rashes hadn't begun popping out—maybe because I realized everyone else was more nervous than I was. I overheard one girl confess she'd spent a year's allowance on her dress. Another, from some modeling school in Virginia, was practically in tears because she couldn't find her coverup stick and she'd just broken a fingernail.

As Ingvild and I began moving closer to the judge's tables, I noticed they looked even more aloof, deadpan, and steely-eyed from up close. I also noticed almost all the other girls had portfolios with terrific eight-by-ten glossies. Had everyone else already spent a fortune on this deal?

"It's not too late to leave," whispered Ingvild.

Maybe so, but I was staying. As pictures of those Lovey Face products flashed across the giant screen, I tried visualizing myself as part of the image. . . . *Me,* splashing on Lovey Face After-Sun Cooler, *me,* smoothing in Lovey Face Tender Blush, spraying on—

"Where are your pictures?" asked the judge.

"Huh?"

"Do you have any photos, dear?" he repeated.

"Photographs? No. Should I?"

The lady in the feathered hat tried being polite. "It would help us to know how you relate to the camera."

"Oh Jenny takes wonderful pictures," said Ingvild, reaching into her wallet. She took out some snapshots Mom had taken of us both clowning around in Riverside Park.

"I didn't know you carried those around," I said.

Some of the shots were really good. There were several of us climbing trees, kicking leaves, and laughing.

"Very sweet," nodded the feathered-hat lady. "You girls both project style and energy. Very nice. Any eight-by-ten glossies?"

We shook our heads.

"Which one is two sixty-five?" asked another judge.

"I am," said Ingvild.

"Do you like sports?" he asked. "We'd like our Lovey Face girl to be active."

Ingvild perked up. "I'm a good skier and I love to skate, too. I like basketball and volleyball and—"

"Very interesting," said the judge, cutting her off. He made some notes on his score sheet, then asked, "Is that your real hair color?"

"Of course. It's even lighter in the summer. Oh, I like to swim, too. And I sew and knit and—well, lots of things."

Now a wispy little lady in a frilly blouse was starting to look me up and down. "Interesting," she said, "but you haven't quite gotten into your look yet, have you dear?"

What was that supposed to mean? Maybe my pants were unzipped or my blouse unbuttoned. Anxiously, I checked all those necessary details, but they seemed okay.

As one of the judges handed the snapshots back to Ingvild, I thought how sweet it was of her to keep them in her wallet, and how glad I was we'd finally cleared the air, and how relieved I was to know she wasn't trying to steal Albert away from me—and how terrific it felt to finally be myself again. Anyway, while I was thinking all this other stuff, I barely heard the judge asking me to take my place up on the runway.

"The what?"

"The *runway,* dear. It's your turn next."

I stared at the girl ahead of me, who was finishing going through her paces on the runway. She had that model's walk down to an art, one foot directly in front of the other, her hips and shoulders swaying from side to side. Her mouth was set in such a permanent toothy smile, it looked like only surgery could remove it from her face. She was wearing a black cashmere circle skirt (which must've cost a thousand dollars) and a slinky black wool sweater.

"That was Number two sixty-three, judges," the announcer called out. "Merri-Lee Matheson from Weston, Connecticut. She's seventeen years old, five feet eight, one hundred and twenty-five pounds. Her favorite sport is horseback riding and she hopes to major in theater when she goes to college."

My mouth hung open as I suddenly realized the announcer must be reading off all that junk we were supposed to have written on our questionnaires. I'd been too preoccupied to notice that before.

"Let's keep things moving, number two sixty-four," snapped one of the judges. "On the runway, please."

Talk about your moment of truth: this seemed to be mine. The very thought of getting up in front of all those people made me want to barf. I didn't have that model's walk or that model's grin or that whole model's attitude, and I hadn't even bothered to finish filling out my questionnaire.

I stood frozen for a second, in a panic.

"Good ahead, Jenny," smiled Ingvild, "you'll be great."

I stared down at my pink jazz shoes, which seemed to have glued themselves to the floor. Then I stared at the photographers, the press corps, the judges, and the hundreds of other girls all staring back at me, waiting. I felt my knees buckling under me, but by some miracle they finally began to function. I slowly moved toward the stage and began walking down the runway. I managed not to fall over my feet, but I couldn't manage a smile. The best I could come up with was a blank stare, which I hoped made me look aloof and sophisticated but probably only succeeded in making me appear subnormal.

"Number two sixty-four," said the announcer at the podium "is Jenny Beaumont from Manhattan. She's five foot four, has blue eyes, and is fifteen years old."

That's all he said, because that's all I'd written down —no hobbies, no interests, no ambitions, nothing. Real exciting, right? When I arrived at the end of the runway— which seemed to take an eternity—I tried to copy that pivot step the girl ahead of me had executed so well. But as I pivoted and turned, my foot hit a seam in the layer of felt and I tripped. I caught myself before I fell, but it could hardly have been considered graceful.

"Thank you, Jenny," said the announcer, "please take a seat."

A seat? I felt like taking a running jump into the nearest river! Suddenly I realized why a person might need seven years of charm school. My heart was pounding so hard, I thought it'd pop out of my chest. I was also breaking out in a sweat, which was leaving charming perspiration stains under the arms of my oversize blouse. I'd rather stick my head in a blender than go through *that* again! How did models do it? How did *Beryl* do it? How can you pretend you're cool and calm and charming while your head's splitting, your stomach's rolling, and your knees are knocking? Amazing!

I also felt a buzz in my ears, so I couldn't even hear what the announcer was saying about Ingvild, who was following close behind me.

"That was awful," she gasped, returning to the seat next to mine. "My legs felt like wood when I got on the stage. I know it was fun for you, Jenny, but I never want to do a thing like that again in my life. I'm not a model and I don't think I want to be one."

"Fun? I nearly *died*. I never want to do it again, either!"

I didn't realize what I'd said until I said it. I mean, for months I'd been looking forward to this deal—scheming, plotting, planning—just so I could get my crack at becoming the Lovey Face girl and be like Beryl. But I wasn't at all like Beryl. Beryl was born to be a model, born to have people stare at her and flash floodlights in her face, born to stand around for hours with the same enchanted expression. For her, it was like eating candy. But I felt like a prize sap, and I was certain I'd looked like one too.

I glanced over at Donna, who was now on the runway swirling her skirt and smiling toward the judges, obviously enjoying every second of attention. That's the sort of girl who should win, I thought, someone who's studied, made the rounds, commuted. Not my sort, who'd done absolutely nothing.

But why hadn't I known that about myself before, for heaven's sake? Clearly, whoever won this competition would have to work real hard at it. There'd be modeling sessions after school and being in bed by nine o'clock all the time, just like Beryl always was. Maybe I could never eat *chocolate* again, either! Suddenly, the whole deal didn't seem so spectacular anymore.

"What are you saying?" asked Ingvild. "If *you* don't want this and *I* don't want this, then what are we *doing* here?"

"What are we doing here?" I repeated, realizing the profundity of the question and the stupidity of my answer: "How should *I* know?"

As Ingvild stared at me blankly, I began laughing. I couldn't help it. I laughed so hard tears started coming to my eyes. Then I got a stabbing pain in my right side, which always happens when I laugh too much.

"Jenny, what's happening?" she asked, patting me on the back. "Please *stop.*"

But I couldn't. It'd turned into a real fit or something, and I couldn't control it.

Donna had just come off the runway and taken her seat next to us. "I hope you're not laughing at *me,*" she said sarcastically, "because I looked great up there."

I shook my head and tried stifling the laughter. "No," I gasped, "I must be laughing at myself." For some weird reason it felt great. What was *wrong* with me, anyhow? I felt as if I'd been waiting to hear details about some terrible disaster and I'd just learned it hadn't actually happened after all. I mean, in a few minutes, somebody's name would be called out over the microphone in the grand ballroom of the Hilton hotel and that girl would go on to become the quintessential Lovey Face image—and I didn't care if that name was mine or not. Well actually, I knew it wouldn't be mine, but I *still* didn't care. In fact, I was relieved. I thought of that line some general was supposed to have said when they tried to get him to run for president: "If nominated, I will not run; if elected, I will not serve." Then I began to laugh again.

The announcer tapped the microphone. "We must ask all contestants to be silent while each girl takes her turn on the runway," he insisted. "The judges will soon be making their decision, and this is an important moment, especially for that fortunate winner."

Right. An important moment for someone. Since I'd just removed myself from the competition, I began wondering who that someone might be: the tall blonde from Virginia who'd won several local beauty pageants? Donna, with her seven years of charm school? Or one of the girls who'd spent a major fortune on photographs? Whoever it was, I assumed she'd be someone who wanted the job desperately—desperately enough to plan, prepare, and *work* for it, all of which I hadn't.

As that thought hit me, I realized it was exactly the type of thing Carolyn would have told me if she'd been around to lecture me about Lovey Face. She probably would've said, "A motivated girl with proper preparation and a positive attitude, not to mention some basic knowledge of modeling's requirements, will undoubtedly win. And that description does not fit you, Jennifer. . . ." Wow, I could actually hear her saying it! And what's worse, it was *true.*

"Are you all right now?" asked Ingvild.

"Sure, I'm my old self again—whoever that is." Except for my emotions, which were giving me a real seesaw ride. I'd stopped laughing; now I felt like *crying.* "Look, let's not wait around to hear them announce the winner, okay? We can sneak out the side door."

"Sneak out? But what if—"

"What if what? One of *us* wins?"

"You're right." She nodded. "Let's go."

We'd barely gotten to the door when pink spotlights began flashing across the stage and the announcer confirmed the judges had selected a winner: "From Rockland County, sixteen-year-old Cassandra Wyman. Cassandra won the Charming Child Contest at age nine, has studied dance for ten years, and hopes to become a choreographer. Her hobbies are tennis, jogging, and sailing. She has ash blond hair, light gray eyes, is five feet . . ."

I heard a loud squeal emerge from somewhere in the center of the ballroom, but I didn't bother checking it out. Cassandra was sure to be poised, confident, and gorgeous. But Ingvild wanted to see her, so she hung back while I rang for the elevator. She caught up with me just before the doors began to close. "She's no prettier than you, Jenny. Taller, but not prettier." When we reached the lobby, she asked, "Are you *sure* you didn't want to win?"

"Maybe just a little bit. How about you?"

"Yes. Maybe a little too. I know I'd make a *terrible* model, but even so."

"Yeah," I agreed gloomily, "even so. Hey, what'll we tell Beryl—and *Liza*. They didn't count on *both* of us failing."

"But we didn't," said Ingvild, putting her arm around my shoulders. "Neither one of us failed today, Jenny."

Well, that's when I really choked up. I mean, when Ingvild said that, I knew *she* knew I felt our friendship was more important than any contest, even though I'd never said it. I also felt she knew all the stupid steps I had to take to finally realize being *myself* was what counted—because she'd gone through all those same sappy steps herself. But neither one of us came right out and said anything like that —that would've been altogether *too* stupid and sappy.

"You're right," I agreed, throwing my arm around her shoulders, "we were *terrific* failures."

Albert called that night. "Wasn't this the big day?"

"That's right."

"Well, what happened?"

"We lost. Both of us."

"Oh. Too bad. Well, better luck next time."

"Next time. Are you *crazed*? I think I'll face facts *now*. I can't sew, I can't cook, I can't ski, I can't get a date with a college jock, and I can't win a modeling contest."

"So what? *I* can't do any of those things either. How about a movie this Sunday? One with sound, okay? I'll pick you up at twelve."

"See you then."

I glanced at myself in the mirror.

Jenny Beaumont, Fairly Ordinary Person, stared back. She wasn't the prettiest, smartest, flashiest, or most popular girl alive, but she had friends who liked her.

I liked her too.

A lot! ·

About the Author

MARY ANDERSON is the author of many novels, including *Catch Me, I'm Falling in Love* and *Do You Call That a Dream Date?* for Delacorte Press. She lives on the Upper West Side of Manhattan with her husband, who is a commercial artist. She has three daughters. She is a native New Yorker and has often used the city as background in her books for young readers.